Davidson King
From These Ashes

From These Ashes

Haven Hart Book 4

Copyright © 2018 : Davidson King

ALL RIGHTS RESERVED

Cover and Interior design by : Designs by Morningstar

Editing done by: Amour The Line Editing

Proofreading provided by: Melissa Womochil and JM Dabney

Interior Design and Formatting provided by Flawless Touch Formatting

The unauthorized reproduction or distribution of this copyrighted work is illegal. No part of this book may be reproduced or transmitted in any form or by any means, including electronic or mechanical means, including photocopying, recording, or by any information storage and retrieval systems, without express written permission from the author, Davidson King. The only exception is in the case of brief quotations embodied in reviews.

This book is a work of fiction. While references may be made to actual places and events, the names, characters, places, and incidents either are products of the author's imagination or are used fictitiously. Any resemblance to actual persons, living or dead, events, or locales is entirely coincidental.

Licensed material is being used for illustrative purposes only and any person depicted in the licensed material is a model.

Other Titles by Davidson King

Haven Hart Series

Snow Falling

Hug It Out

A Dangerous Dance

Collaborations:

The Hunt~ Co-Authored with JM Dabney

Trademarks

All products and/or band names mentioned are registered trademarks of their respective holders/companies.

WARNINGS

This book is intended for people 18 years or older. There is sensitive material such as: sex, off page abuse, on page domestic abuse, off page self-harm, and graphic violence.

DEDICATION

I am absolutely dedicating this book to everyone in my reader's group. You all endured months of teasers waiting for Black and Quill! You pushed me, supported me, and loved me through it. Thank you so much.

CHAPTER ONE

Black

Living a life in the shadows wasn't easy. To many, they only saw a certain persona. To the rest, I was something completely different. My father used to say we lived in an optical illusion. I didn't agree with him when I was younger, but I did now.

One side of my life was the current Hell I was in at this very moment. A fundraiser gala. It was to help support the pediatric cardiology department at Hart's Hope Hospital. I didn't mind the tuxedo as I often favored suits. I didn't really mind my date, Teresa, who looked stunning in her crimson red, floor-length gown, matching shoes, and more diamonds twinkling against her skin than a Tiffany's display case. It was how fake they all felt they had to be. No one was genuinely selfless. We all wanted what was best for us first and foremost, and donating ridiculous amounts of money we never wanted to part with was how we made everyone love us.

"Isn't that Richard Franklin?" Teresa asked as she sipped her champagne. Her blue eyes were homed in on the multi-millionaire who sat at a table with many other rich people of Haven Hart.

"I believe so. Why don't you go say hello while I grab another drink at the bar?" I knew Teresa was only here to network and that didn't offend me. I knew I'd be fucking her by the end of the night and she'd be gone by morning. That was a win for me. Great sex and no small talk.

"Are you sure?" Her golden hair was up in a relaxed bun,

giving her an almost girl-next-door appearance, but the rest of her was all glamour, sex, and money.

"I'm positive. Go schmooze so I don't have to. I will be over at the bar when you're ready to leave."

I had told her I wasn't a fan of these things and would love a buffer. Teresa, a low woman on the totem pole PR agent, was desperate for her big break. I didn't trust my secrets and lies to anyone, and I had told her as much. But I liked her enough to see if I could get her a client or two that could help her business.

I watched her saunter across the dance floor, smiling as she purposely bumped into any gentleman she could. Each man's eyes lingered over her curvy form and by the time she reached her target, many men were drooling and many women were scowling.

The bar was long and wide, which suited me well. I didn't like being squished and forced to be polite to people due to close quarters. I ordered a drink, sat on the mahogany stool, smoothed my beard down, and scanned the room.

There were two sides to every coin. To every person in this room, I was Terrance Blackrose, owner of Red Rose Protection Agency. I offered security and protection to the most elite. If you could afford it, you were elite to me. To the rest of the world, I was Black. I ran an assassin organization for the darkest and most powerful people in the world. One side of my life protected, the other killed.

Teresa was laughing beside Richard, and I was glad she had made a connection. It was close to the end of the gala and I was starving. I could never eat those tiny morsels they offered and feel filled. I wanted to grab a bite, go home, fuck Teresa into the mattress, and pass out.

Like she could sense my need, she got up, said farewell to Richard, and walked over to me, a bright smile challenging any other in the room.

"Are you ready to go?" she whispered into my ear, her breasts pressed against my arm, and I wondered if I was really as hungry as I had previously thought.

"I am." I placed the tumbler on the bar and wrapped my arm around her waist. The gala was clearing out and I nodded my farewell to some people I knew. We stood under the large awning as limos and luxury cars lined up.

For events, I opted for my Cadillac SUV stretched limousine. It was on the obnoxious side, but I liked the comfort it provided. I wasn't a small man. At over six foot five inches, I was tall. Because I worked out so much, I was also broad, muscular, and as some said, a monster. I needed room. It also helped that all my vehicles were armored. Teresa knew I ran a protection agency, she didn't know I had a target on my back because of my other occupation.

"Here you go, sir," the valet said with a smile as he held the door open. He was cute with his auburn hair, blue eyes, and sexy smirk. If Teresa hadn't been with me, I'd have offered him a ride, and not just in my car.

"I'm starving," Teresa said after my driver hit the highway.

"Why don't we stop somewhere? I didn't eat much, I rarely do at these things."

Her laughter sounded like wind chimes. "Same here. It's all rabbit food." She reached into her clutch and pulled out her phone. "It's not even midnight yet, I could go for a meatball sub and I love Quirks and Perks sandwiches. Want to stop there?"

I'd eaten at that place a couple times since I had been introduced to it a few months ago. I enjoyed the food and the atmosphere. The barista, Quill, on the other hand, was a challenge. There was an appeal that niggled at me with every glance, but he was young, flirty, and dangerous.

"Whatever you want," I answered as I sat back and made quick work of answering a few emails and texts. Jones, one of my assassins, was in Brazil hunting a drug smuggler who gave a

British debutant some bad shit, causing a drug overdose. Her father had gone on a rampage and wanted everyone killed. He'd contacted me, and I was able to make him understand that cutting the head of the snake off would be the best retaliation. He wanted to send a message. Jones, also known as Hangman, was perfect for the job. He'd kill the drug lord and hang his body for all to see. The text from him had confirmed the job was done and I was able to let the father know.

"We're here," Teresa said as we pulled up to the curb.

My driver opened the car door, and I chuckled as Teresa slipped off her shoes and walked barefoot into the café. The fact it was frigid outside didn't stop her.

It was practically empty, there was a young couple sitting on a loveseat in the corner and an old man at a two-seater sipping his coffee. I only saw a young woman at the counter and breathed a sigh of relief when Quill was nowhere in sight. A part of me sort of enjoyed seeing what shenanigans he'd be up to, the other part couldn't be bothered.

"What can I get you?" the woman, Melissa, asked.

"I would like a meatball sub and a water. I'd have coffee, but then I'd never sleep." Teresa gave a very uninterested Melissa her everybody-loves-me smile.

"Can I have your burger sub with extra pickles and mayo and a large iced coffee?" I didn't sleep much, so coffee or not, it wouldn't matter.

"That'll be fifteen sixty." I handed her my card and signed when she gave me the receipt. "Quill, I have an order. Don't clean the grills yet," Melissa shouted, and I cringed. Not because she was loud, but because Quill was, in fact, working and, in that moment, I wasn't ready to see him.

"Okay." His voice came from the back and I silently hoped he wouldn't come up front.

While we waited, Teresa went on and on about Richard and

how great he was and that he had told her he'd call her on Monday for an appointment. I wasn't really listening to what she said and was glad when Melissa handed me my iced coffee so I could go over to the DIY counter to fix it.

"Here you go." I heard Quill's voice and stupidly thought if I didn't turn around, he wouldn't see me. But the kid had me on some kind of radar.

"Well, hello there," he purred, and the sound of his footsteps told me he was coming my way. "Late night I see?"

I turned in his direction since there was no point in trying to run, he was relentless. "I had a work thing. Do you always work late?"

He shrugged as he fixed the sugar packets. His wrist was covered in his usual bracelets and his nails were painted a ruby red. "Sometimes. I have many jobs, as you know."

I did. A couple months ago, Quill had witnessed one of my former assassins, Mace, put a bullet in a guy's head. Bill, who was working with Mace at the time, didn't want to off the kid, so I had them drive him to my office. It was there I learned that while annoying, Quill was loyal to a fault. I should have killed him, but his eyes told a tale older than his twenty-two years. I offered him a job to keep tabs on him. When I needed something delivered that wasn't on the up and up, Quill made the item get to its destination. I rarely got to see him, and that was just fine by me. He seemed a bit obsessed with me.

"I'll bring the tray over to the booth," Teresa said as she walked past me.

"That your girlfriend?" I looked up in time to see Quill's sour expression. It was short-lived though, and he smiled wide when he met my gaze. I didn't know his eye color. Every time I saw him, he had different contacts in. Today they were violet.

"A date for the evening if you really must know." I placed the lid on my coffee and walked in the direction of my food.

"A date that isn't a girlfriend? So, you're still single?" I heard Quill following me and, by the amused expression on Teresa's face as I approached the booth, she had heard Quill's question.

"Quill, I need you to clean the grill so we can close at a reasonable time tonight," Melissa said. She gave Quill a small smile that told me she wasn't angry, but there was something else there. I didn't know what their relationship was, but when Quill went over to her, she squeezed his shoulder.

As soon as Quill was out of sight, she shot me a venomous glare. It was like ice in my veins. She was not happy with me and I didn't have a clue why. I hadn't done anything.

"So good," Teresa said around her bite of food.

"Hurry up with that. I've been dying to get you out of that dress all evening." I winked at her as she blushed and laughed as she began eating much faster.

I couldn't worry about Quill, he was more than half my age and we had nothing in common. The fact he now worked for me meant he was off limits. I didn't need more drama than what my life already had.

I didn't see Quill again and when Teresa and I slipped back into my limo, I was ready for dessert. By the salacious look she gave me, I knew she was too.

Chapter Two

Quill

"Why do you always do this to yourself?" Melissa asked me as we closed up the café. I knew she was talking about my flirting with Black. I loved Melissa to pieces and knew she wasn't being cruel in thinking I was wasting my time, she was just worried about me.

"I'm totally going to wear that man down, you'll see. You'll all see," I shouted comically with my fists raised to the sky. Her laugh lightened the moment and I gave her a sideways hug as we walked toward her car.

"I get a bad vibe from the guy, is all." She clicked the fob on her keys and I slipped into the passenger side. Melissa was a worrier and yes, she had every reason to worry about me. I had bad taste in men and bad luck.

"Just because he's as big as Thor and richer than God doesn't mean he's Satan." I chuckled at all those comparisons. Thor, God, and Satan… hmm, maybe he was a combination.

"That is not why I am saying that." She started the car and blasted the heat. It was the beginning of December and freaking freezing. Normally, I'd walk the five blocks to the bus and take it back to my fabulously shitty apartment. But, Melissa always argued, so now I just let her drop me off.

"Mel, he's hot. He's every wet dream I've had since I realized my dick pointed to other dicks. He rejects me every time anyway, so don't worry about him hurting me. He'd have to actually touch me to hurt me." And wasn't that a sobering thought? I wasn't used to soft touches unless it was Mel hugging me or taking care of me after my many mistakes.

"I dunno, Quill." She didn't say any more about Black, and for that, I was glad. I knew he'd reject me each time, but playing this game was always fun. It took me out of my depressing headspace and onto a whole different plane of existence.

When she pulled in front of my place, she wouldn't unlock the door. I followed her gaze and saw the dark Mustang sitting in the unused driveway beside the complex.

"What's he doing here?" she asked, still not unlocking the doors. "Why don't you stay at my place tonight? My brother isn't home, you can take his room or the couch." She was frantic to get me to go home with her, but as soon as the driver's side door of the Mustang opened, I knew it was too late.

"I'll be fine, Mel." I leaned across the middle and gave her a kiss on the cheek. Quickly, I reached over and hit the unlock button, and before she could lock me in, I opened my door.

"Call me in one hour," she shouted out her open window. "You hear me? One hour or I call the cops."

I just shook my head and waved her away as I made my way up the steps to the entrance of the building. It wasn't a huge apartment complex. Three floors and, of course, I was on the top and the elevator didn't work. But three floors were no big deal.

I had just opened the front door of the building when I heard his steps speed up behind me.

"Why would she want you to call her and why is she threatening to call the cops?" he asked as he pushed the door open farther so I couldn't close it on him.

Mel's car was gone, and I was glad she wasn't here. I knew this conversation wasn't going to go well. I'd been avoiding him, and it was only a matter of time before he caught up with me.

"What do you want, Ronnie?" I knew what he wanted, and he knew I knew. A part of me wanted to turn on my heels and march up the stairs to my apartment, but I really didn't want him in there with me.

"Let's go upstairs and talk." He loomed over me. I wasn't big, not even average. My mother drank and smoked while she was pregnant with me and I was born premature and in bad shape. I was always the tiny kid in school. Fortunately, never sickly, but I was only five foot four. I didn't have muscles like Black. Melissa called me lithe, but that was her being nice.

Ronnie, on the other hand, was big, tall, and by the look in his dark eyes, angry. When I had first met him, I was naturally attracted to the dark interest he showed me. He was always so clean and sharp. At first, he was even charming. Then, like most of my relationships, he showed his true colors.

"I left you a message, Ronnie. I don't think we should see each other anymore." I was proud of myself for not stuttering and keeping eye contact.

"Is that right?" He gripped my arm and a ripple of pain shot all the way up to my shoulder. "I think we need to go upstairs and talk about this properly." He pressed his lips against mine painfully, never releasing my arm. He bit down hard and I could taste the blood... my blood.

"Ron... Ronnie." Now, I did stutter and when he smirked, I knew he was loving how afraid he was making me.

"Now, Quill." He pushed me and I slammed into the metal trash can in the lobby, sparks of pain bursting through my back. When I fell onto my other arm, the hurt was vicious, and Ronnie laughed.

"Get the fuck up, you clumsy shit." He reached down and wrenched me up by my shirt. This time when he pushed me, it was toward the stairs.

Each step made me crawl deeper inside of myself. There was a place I hid where no one could get to me. Not the Ronnies, my shitty family, nor all the bullies I had dealt with in school growing up. It was so dark there. It muffled the words spewed at me; it softened the blows. It numbed everything.

When we got inside my apartment, it didn't take Ronnie long to remind me why I wanted nothing to do with him anymore. He grabbed my head and like a ball, slammed it against the wall. Bright lights flashed in front of my closed lids and tendrils of agony danced around my brain.

"You don't leave me, Quill." When I slid to the floor, I wrapped my arm around myself to try to block his kick, but all I managed to do was make him angrier. He clutched my hair to bring my face inches from his. "You're mine, get it? Or do you need more reminding?"

I shook my head as best I could in his grip. "I got it."

"Now get your ass in the bedroom and I'll help you to not forget what you are."

I didn't cry anymore. I think the last time I cried, I was eleven and my father had been killed by some neighborhood gang because he wouldn't change the colors of his bakery. It was something ridiculous. I had cried that night. But never again.

That didn't mean I didn't want to, I just didn't see the point in it and had convinced myself it was unnecessary.

When I was somewhat steady on my feet, I started shuffling toward the bedroom when someone banged on the door, freezing me in the moment.

"Quill Almeida, this is the Haven Hart Police. We received a call about a domestic dispute. Please open up."

Ronnie looked at me with a rage that had me cowering. "That fucking bitch really did call the cops?"

Knowing Mel, she had.

"Mr. Almeida, open the door."

Ronnie stalked over to the door and opened it a crack so they wouldn't see me.

"Good evening, officers," Ronnie said in a respectful tone.

"Are you Quill Almeida?" I heard an officer ask.

"No, I'm Ronald Sterling, his boyfriend." Hearing that last name, I was sure the officers would leave. The Sterling family was a growing power in Haven Hart. They were always in the news for giving to needy charities. Ronnie's father, Bartholomew Sterling, was the ambassador of generosity and the Sterling family was well loved in this city.

"I see," the officer said. "Is Quill Almeida here? We received a call from someone saying there was a fight. They said they saw someone harming Mr. Almeida."

"Hmm." All I could see was Ronnie's profile, and he was pretending to think. "No, he isn't here. Maybe they thought they saw something. I can tell you, I was just moving the couch and knocked over a lamp. Perhaps that's what they heard?"

What so much of Haven Hart didn't know about the Sterlings was how they were master manipulators, abusers, and royal pieces of shit. I knew if those cops left, not even my safe, dark place was going to stop Ronnie from taking a chunk out of me. I knew what I was about to do would only buy me some time, but I did it anyway.

"Help!" I shouted. Ronnie's head turned toward me, a half-shocked look on his face.

"Move out of the way, Mr. Sterling," the cop ordered, much angrier at this point, and pushed the door open. "Shit." He raced over to me while the other cop stood by Ronnie.

"Mr. Almeida, I'm Officer Drakes. I'm calling an ambulance." He looked over to his partner. "Take him downstairs."

I listened as Officer Drake's partner read Ronnie his rights and breathed painfully when he was gone. As the adrenaline left my body, the crushing pain weighed down on me.

I closed my eyes as the officer asked me questions. I zoned out as the paramedics poked and prodded me, and then drifted to my dark place where even after all of this, I still didn't cry.

I used to wish to be saved. When I was younger and lay in my bed starving because there was no money for food since my mom or brother had pissed it away, or when I had been between apartments after being evicted because I couldn't pay rent, I had wished for a prince to sweep me up and take me far, far away. He never came, so I gave up on that dream.

As I was wheeled into the emergency room of Hart's Hope Hospital, I found myself wishing for it one more time. Maybe this time, my prince would come.

Chapter Three

Black

"Thank you, Lana." Lana Davis was my personal assistant and while I didn't trust a soul, she was the closest thing to a sister or confidant I had. She handled both sides of my life without question. Part of it had a lot to do with the fact that when she was ten, my father orchestrated her rescue from a shipping crate headed to the other side of the world. Lana felt she owed my family forever and for that, she was privy to more than most.

"You're welcome. You really should eat better and this morning as I was making my salad, I figured it wouldn't kill me to make a little extra for you." She shrugged, and I knew it was due, in part, to the fact she was thinking about her own loneliness.

That was a common thing in our practice. I had no living family anymore, and when I had taken over my father's business, I refused to bring anyone into it. My life, while filled with luxuries, was also dangerous.

A former assassin I had, Riordan Darcy, worked for me for over fifteen years. His family was a weakness for him and I often told him it would be what would make him crumble. Enemies prey on your soft spots. But Teddy owned Riordan's heart, and what they had gone through just to have love made me jealous. I had never wanted anyone until I saw them together.

But I wasn't Riordan. I wasn't like any one of the people who worked under me. I was the leader and my destruction would ruin it all. They'd take out anyone I loved, and I couldn't lose my heart... not again.

"I have another charity dinner before Christmas, the one for the orphanage. Why don't you join me?"

Lana's head shot up in surprise. "Really?" I had never invited her to them because I usually brought whomever I wanted to fuck. But Lana looked like she could really use this. Lana didn't get the mean side of who I was. Many saw me and thought I was terrifying or mysterious. But when you have practically grown up with someone, it was hard to be big, bad Black with them.

"Absolutely. Use the company card to get a dress, shoes, do your hair, and all that glamorous stuff." I finished my salad and pushed the empty plate to the side and wiped my mouth.

"Okay." She smiled brightly. "Thank you, Terry."

That was another thing. Whenever it was just Lana and me, she called me Terry. She had known me since I was fifteen, and grew up seeing me rise to the seat I was betrothed to. Seeing as she was ten at the time, she had always looked up to me and I didn't want to let her down where I could.

"You're welcome."

My phone interrupted us and when I saw it was another former employee, I couldn't help but smile. Lana grabbed our plates and left my office.

"What's the matter, Mace, you realized Bill wasn't worth it and you want me to help hide you?" I answered, smiling wider when he laughed.

"No. Bill is good. So very good."

Mace was one of my best assassins. A couple of months ago, he had taken on a job for mob boss Christopher Manos and was teamed up with one of his guys, Bill. They had managed to complete their mission of destroying any trace of the Marks family and the president of crazy, Zagan Marks. Unfortunately, Mace didn't get out unscathed. He had lost a finger, had a scar across his forehead, and wasn't the same. It hurt to let him go after our history, but it was for the best. He was still in recovery, but he was doing it at Christopher's mansion with Bill at his side.

"I don't want to know about your activities. What can I do for you, Mace?"

"Word's not out that I'm not tied to you anymore and I got a call from some guy saying he's at the docks. There was a package that needed to be picked up, but your guy never showed."

Fucking dammit, Quill. "Is he still there?"

"Yeah, he said he'd be there for another thirty minutes. You want me...?" I had to stop him there. This wasn't his life anymore.

"No. I'll handle it." There was a long silence and I knew Mace was thinking I didn't think him capable. "Mace," I whispered. "Enjoy your life. We don't all get to have one." I didn't wait for a response. I hung up.

"Lana?" I yelled, knowing she was right by my door.

"Yes?" She stood in the doorway, phone in hand.

"Make sure to disconnect Mace from all communication, and then get me Quill. I want his ass in my office in an hour. And tell Lee to get to the docks to get a package. He has twenty to get there." She was already dialing before I had finished talking.

I hadn't sent Quill on a lot of jobs, but he never fucked up. I was already thinking this was a bad idea hiring him on, but every time I was ready to just tell him to forget it, he'd look at me with those color-of-the-day eyes and I'd just let him have the win. Now? Not so much. Fucking up wasn't something I tolerated.

Lana strolled into my office, reading something off her phone. "Lee is en route, Mace is disconnected, but... um." She looked up and her expression wasn't the confident one I was used to.

"What, is Quill on his way?"

"No." She held up her hand, halting my tirade. "I tried his cell, there was no answer, so I called over to Quirks and Perks. A woman named Melissa said he didn't work today and wouldn't talk further about it. Then I called his other job…"

"What other job?" I assumed when Quill said he had other jobs, he was referring to the one he worked for me.

"He also works at Joker's Sin part-time."

What the fuck? Why did he work so many jobs? He was a single guy. What had him working at a gay nightclub, and what was he doing there?

"Fine. Is he there?"

She shook her head. "I… Well, I spoke to his boss, Atlas. Sir, Quill is in the hospital."

I thought back to when I had seen Quill a few nights ago at Quirks and Perks. He had seemed fine. His normal, annoying self. He hadn't looked sick or anything. Which meant something had happened to him.

"Why?" I could hear the growl in my own voice.

"He said he didn't know, but I think it's safe to assume he won't make his deliveries for the next few days and he won't be able to get here today." There was a sadness in Lana's expression, and I knew she was worried.

She liked Quill. Most everyone did. Whenever he came by to get paid or something, she told me he always brought her a dessert and a coffee without asking. He gave her make up tips and often times gossiped with her about what was happening in the celebrity world.

When she glanced out the window, I could tell she was ready to cry. Fucking shit.

"Have my driver bring the car around. I'll go down to the hospital and find out what's going on." Just like that, Lana smiled, and I wondered when I had become such a sucker.

With my leather coat in hand, I left my office. Lana accompanied me all the way down, helping me rearrange my schedule since my whole day was now fucked up. I got in the car and instructed the driver to take me to Hart's Hope Hospital.

It didn't take all that long to get there, and when I did, I went directly to the information desk and asked for Quill Almeida's room. It seemed anyone could just go up and see him, and I wasn't thrilled with the hospital's security.

I told my driver to stay in the lobby and took the elevator to the floor Quill was on.

My phone rang as I was walking down the corridor to his room. "What is it, Lee?"

"I got the package. Where's it going?"

"Send it to…" I had just walked into Quill's room and briefly forgot what I was going to say when my eyes landed on his battered body. It was like someone had hit me in the chest with a wrecking ball. "Lee, Lana has the address. Call her, then get your ass to Hart's Hope."

I disconnected and took a few steps closer to Quill. His expression was defiant, and he stared me down like he was daring me.

"What happened to you?" I asked, taking in his black and blue face, his arm wrapped in what seemed to be a cast, and… It was in that moment, I realized his eyes were devoid of contacts. "Your eyes, they're green. Is that your real color?"

"First off, yes they are really green and second, I found out the hard way that a sword fight with a narwhal is a bad idea. Clearly, I need guidance in the world of adulting."

"Games. I see." I leaned over Quill, my face an inch from his. "I rearranged my whole day for this, so let's play."

CHAPTER FOUR

Quill

Black's eyes glowed as he hovered only a few inches from my face. I could smell his aftershave and a sort of spiciness I couldn't quite place. The fact he was in my hospital room both stunned and embarrassed me. I should be shocked he'd found me, but I knew finding people was something this man was very good at. But why did he care if I was here at all?

"Explain to me, Quill, why exactly you're in a hospital bed?" The timbre of his voice vibrated up my spine. I wanted to tell him, but I knew it would make me look weak. To a man like Black, letting someone beat the shit out of you because you were too afraid to fight back would be pathetic. What Black didn't know, what he couldn't, was that unless you could kill them, fighting back was simply dragging out the inevitable.

"It's winter, Black, I was climbing the steps to get into my building and I fell. My shit landlord didn't salt the steps." When he narrowed his eyes, I knew he was trying to sniff out the lie.

"How many steps is it into your building?"

Weird question. "Three, maybe four, why?"

When he huffed, his breath wafted over me. Mint and whiskey.

"I'd believe the arm, maybe, but the conveniently placed bruises on your face? No. You're lying to me. Why?" He stood to his full height. A blond, beautiful giant. Thor and Satan for sure. I loved his long hair glittering like strands of gold. He always wore it in a braid, and tiny flecks of gray peeked through. I always wanted to pull the tie out and see it free-flowing. I would bet it was like a silky mane, and with his sculpted beard, he was as mighty and glorious as a lion. *Oh, for fuck's sake, what kind of drugs was I on?*

"I'm not lying," I said with as much conviction as I could muster. The headache I had almost gotten rid of began to surface again.

"When did this 'tumble' happen?" He used air quotes for tumble, and for a minute, I thought the sarcasm was a little out of place for him.

"Night before last. Yeah, I think that's right?" I tried thinking what day of the week it was. Atlas had called me yesterday, and I told him I couldn't work and why, and he said fine so…

"The night I saw you at Quirks and Perks?" An adorable look of confusion adorned his face and I sort of wanted to squish his cheeks.

"Yeah." I nodded. The smile he gave me was one of victory. I had fucked up somehow.

"It just started snowing last night. Before that, there hasn't been snow or rain for over a week." He pointed an accusing finger at me. "Stop lying."

"I am not lying." My voice raised and I was about to go into a terrific and believable story when Lee, one of Black's men, walked in.

"He's lying," Lee stated barely above a whisper, but it was heard loud and clear.

"How the hell do you know? And why are you even here?" I was getting indignant and my head was officially pounding.

"How do you know he's lying?" Black addressed Lee, who rolled his eyes as if insulted by the question.

"When you instructed me to come here, I called Lana like you told me to. She gave me the address to drop off the package, we can talk about why it was delivered to a top-notch cardiologist later, and then she asked if while I was going to the hospital if I was visiting Quill."

The package. Of course, that was why Black was here. I was supposed to have gone to the dock to pick up a delivery. It wasn't me he was worried about, he wanted to know why I was in a hospital bed because I hadn't done my job.

"I asked Lana what she was talking about and she filled me in best she could. So, I took a cab on my way here so I could do a little digging." Lee continued like he wasn't destroying my entire reputation to Black.

"Did you now?" Black gave me a smirk I half wanted to smack but mostly wanted to lick.

"Two nights ago, Ronald Sterling, son of Bartholomew Sterling, was arrested for domestic assault. Normally, domestic disputes are a dime a dozen, but not for the Sterling family. However, I stumbled upon that information after contacting Quill's landlord." Lee spoke as if I wasn't even in the room, and I wanted to scream.

"Get to the point, Lee, please." While Lee wouldn't look at me, Black wouldn't take his eyes off me, and it was strange. I wanted this man's undivided attention all the time, but right then, in the glare of his judgement, not so much.

"Two nights ago, there was a call to Quill's place for a domestic disturbance, and you can guess the rest." Lee waved his hand in a yadda yadda way. "I'm assuming you called me down here to find all this out to begin with, and since I have and I've told you, should I be going?"

"Hold on." Black held his hand up, silencing Lee. "Why are you still in the hospital? Usually, they patch people up and send them on their way."

Yeah, and all the times I'd been to the hospital, it was normally what they did. "I have, well, had a concussion. I'm being discharged today."

"But still, you can be discharged for a concussion," Lee added, and I really wanted him to leave.

"Can you go now?" I asked the man who seemed to want to scram just as much as I wanted him to.

"Quill, allow me to explain everything to you," Black began. I watched as he grabbed a chair and slid it beside my bed, then sat. "I'm guessing you had no one at home to wake you hourly, and that is one reason they kept you. I'm also guessing it's not your first concussion, and that worries doctors a lot as well." He was exactly right. He sat cool as ever, hands folded on his lap, regarding me.

"Maybe," I said.

"Lee, where is this Ronald Sterling now?"

"Out on bail," he said, bored.

"I see." Black's eyes scanned over my body. The intensity of it all made it feel like it was his hands. I wished it was. "Lee will be going to your place and setting up security for you when…"

Lee interrupted Black, and for a minute, I thought Black was going to shoot him for the disrespect.

"I don't mean to interrupt, but I can't do that."

Black scoffed at Lee. "You can and you will."

"No, sir, I can't, because when I spoke to the landlord today, he explained that Quill wasn't welcome back. Because he has a weekly lease with him, it expired yesterday. He can't return. He did say he will keep the apartment unrented for a week, giving him time to remove his belongings." Lee began scrolling through his phone, searching for what, I didn't know. All I could think about was the fact I had lost another place to live.

"I will speak with this landlord. If he wants Quill out, that's fine, but he will give him enough time to find another place. Text me his number. In the meantime, Lee, go and look around Quill's apartment and prepare a security plan. When I'm done with the landlord, Quill will be able to stay there." Lee nodded and left.

"You do know my landlord will be making my life miserable if you force him to keep me there. You get that, right?" I didn't know why Black was caring at all what happened to me, probably because he needed me back to doing his deliveries.

"No. He won't." Black's phone vibrated, likely the text he was waiting for, and then he put his phone to his ear. I watched transfixed as he spoke to my asshole landlord.

"Good morning, are you the landlord for the property, The Fielding Complex? Wonderful, then you're who I need to speak with. My name is Terrance Blackrose of..." There was a silence, and I sat there with my mouth agape. Terrance Blackrose? Many months ago, and anytime since, I'd look at the credit cards he used, but there was never anything on there except Red Rose Securities. Terrance... Yeah, I could see it. I knew I was smiling, and when Black narrowed his eyes at me, I also knew it was his way of telling me to knock it off.

"Yes, of Red Rose Securities. One of my men was staying in one of your apartments, Quill Almeida..." Another pause. I knew my shitty landlord, Lenny, was telling Black how horrible I was. "I don't really care what your opinion is of my employee. I do care that you illegally evicted him while he is laid up in the hospital. Now, if you know who I am, you know that I'm not going to let that just go. So let me tell you what you're going to do next. You're going to leave Quill the hell alone. He will be allowed to stay there, paying rent, until he's ready to vacate the premises. If at any time his stay there is unpleasant, or you talk to him even to say hello, you will be greeted with swift force. You're somewhat smart. I'm sure you can figure out what I mean by that, yes?"

I didn't know anything that happened after that. I stared, stunned and speechless, as Black, without raising his voice once, put my landlord in his place.

"There. Now you can stay at your place. Lee will set up your security. When you're all healed, you and I will have another chat."

I still couldn't talk. I wanted to climb him like a tree, wrap myself around his body, and never let go.

"Speak words, Quill."

It wasn't until he touched my hand that I regained my ability to talk.

"I want to lick your whole body." Yep, those were the words I spoke. *Awesome. Go me.*

Chapter Five

Black

As I stared at Quill lying in that hospital bed, flirting like it was just another day, I wondered if he thought he was fooling others. He wasn't fooling me. While that was typical Quill, it was also an avoidance technique. I had no doubt he was attracted to me, I'd be an idiot not to see it, but I was sure a lot of his snarkiness and flirty behavior was a front.

"Okay, Quill, the doctor signed your discharge papers... Oh, hello, I'm Nurse Kathy, are you a friend of my buddy Quill here?" The petite, blonde nurse asked, and the whole thing didn't feel right.

"I'm his boss," I stated in a clipped tone. The nurse was too friendly to have just met Quill.

"Oh, it's nice to see someone other than Mel come to visit him." She patted Quill's blanket-covered leg, and I suddenly wanted to grill him. How many times had he been in here to be on such good terms with the medical staff?

"Quill is being discharged now?"

She nodded. "That's right. Is Mel coming to get you, sweetie?"

Quill's gaze shifted from me to Kathy, then to the door. "Um, no, I will call an Uber."

Like fuck he was taking an Uber. "No. I'll be driving him home."

For a minute, I thought Quill was going to interrupt but after one look at me, he shut his mouth. I wasn't arguing about this.

"That's terrific. Let me just go over his discharge instructions with you, so—" Kathy began to explain to me, and I was eager to hear what she had to say when Quill interrupted, his aggravation obvious.

"No! He's just my boss. It's not his business. And I know what to do, Kathy."

I had never heard Quill angry, and the quiver of fear that laced his words was worrisome.

"I'm sorry, honey, I wasn't going to tell him your history. Just how to make your recovery better, but it's your choice. I'll just ask you to leave so I can go over this with Quill." I'd seen that sympathy before. She wanted to help Quill, but he didn't want any. I went to leave, but left Quill with a parting word.

"You've been trying to get my attention for months, Quill. Well, now you have it. You'll see exactly what that entails now."

Right before the door closed, I heard his gasp and almost chuckled.

WHILE THERE WAS a certain amount of dampened demeanor to Quill, it didn't stop him from touching every button and gadget in my car.

"Wow, you can have heat on the left and AC on the right?" His eyes were wide with wonder and it was funny how something so minor lit him up.

"Yes, but it's winter, so can you knock it off?" I hit the AC button to turn it off and was pleased when Quill stopped touching everything.

"You didn't have to take me home," he whispered as he stared out the window.

"I'm aware. You didn't have to lie to me, but here we are." My phone vibrated with a text from Lee.

"It's not a lie if I just don't tell you anything."

He sounded like a child, but he pretty much was, wasn't he? Twenty-two; damn, I remembered that age too well.

"An omission is still a lie in my book, Quill." He blew a raspberry at my comment.

"You sound like an angry dad." When he was silent for too long, I glanced at him. His green eyes were on me, and fuck if he wasn't in flirt mode. "Wanna be my angry daddy?"

"No."

With a quirk of his brow, he kept going. "We can play detention. Oh no, Mr. Black, I didn't mean to smoke in the bathroom. Maybe if you had something better to put in my mouth, I would—"

"Please stop." We couldn't reach his place fast enough.

"Or maybe doctor. You can assess my whole body, maybe—"

That gave me the opening I needed. "And what, Quill? I'd be able to actually see what that piece of shit did to you? Would you open up to me then and stop the lies and games?"

He didn't flinch when I leaned into him, but the flirtiness was gone; in its place, defiance.

"Would you?" he bit back. "Would you open up, *Terrance*?"

"We're here," my driver spoke through the speaker. It didn't break our staring contest. I had underestimated Quill. He was a lot stronger than I thought.

"No, Quill, and that's the last time you say my name. Understand me?"

"I understand a lot, Black. More than I think even you do, but I am curious what having your attention will mean for me? Do we have Sunday dinners now? I make a yummy taco dip. Or was that all for Kathy's approval? Work the staff and they'll all love you?" His smile was full of sarcasm. "I know that maneuver. Look good for everyone else, but when the door shuts, you turn into—"

"You know nothing, Quill. Nothing about me. Never think for a second I'd ever be like Ronald Sterling. Never ever think that.

Of all the horrors I've rained down on people, none were undeserving."

Our conversation was cut short when my driver opened the door for Quill.

"Thank you for the ride, Boss." Quill slipped out and I opened my side door, ready to follow him up.

"No, Black. I don't want you in my place. I have a say, right? You said as much a few seconds ago." He wouldn't turn and face me. He held his small, clear bag of belongings from the hospital tight to his chest. I saw Lee standing by the entrance to his complex.

"Lee is inside. He will show you how the security works."

I watched as he entered the building. Lee waved me off. Had Lee not been there, no amount of pushing would have stopped me from entering Quill's place.

I hated how familiar this whole situation was. I hated more that Quill would compare me to someone like Ronald Sterling. The anger was so intense, I felt it like fire in my veins.

Dialing Jones, I decided the Sterlings needed to understand Quill was off limits.

"Yeah?" Jones' voice was his typical deep, gravelly, and disconnected.

"I want you following Ronald Sterling for me. Tomorrow, you, Lee, and I will be paying him a visit."

"You got it." He hung up, and I tried to calm myself down.

Hours later, I found myself still unable to get Quill out of my head.

CHAPTER SIX

Quill

"I'm going to make this very simple for you," Lee said as I shut my apartment door. I immediately noticed the mess from when Ronnie attacked me was gone.

"Did you clean?"

"No. Now please pay attention, I don't enjoy repeating myself." I watched as he walked over to the small table beside my TV and lifted a little black box. I wanted to ask him about my apartment and who had cleaned it up, but he started talking again. And because I didn't want to inadvertently summon the fire department by hitting the wrong thing, I listened.

"There are three buttons in here. The blue one sets the system up. You hit it, it all turns on. You hit it again, it turns off. Don't turn it off." Lee was nerd-scary. I felt like he could make the world burn with a switch.

"The white one arms your defense, so..."

"Whoa." I had to stop him. "Arms my defense? What the hell have you done to my apartment?"

Lee rolled his eyes as if my question wasn't a good one. It was a great one. "We are monitoring you around the clock. Small cameras are in place everywhere, minus the bathroom. If we see something, we will come. You hit the white button when you're leaving or going to sleep. Whenever you or your place will be most vulnerable. It's programmed to avoid your DNA, so don't feel like you can't walk around your apartment when you hit it."

I had to sit down. "I have so many questions, Lee."

"Hold them until the end. Now, the red one is the 'holy shit' button. You hit this and everyone is notified. Black, the police, fire, ambulance. You name it. Whoever gets here first wins." He smiled creepily and while I marveled at the technology, I was worried too.

"What do the defenses do and how'd you get my DNA?"

Lee shut the box and placed it on the couch beside me. "I'm very good at what I do, Quill. I don't much believe in guns coming down from the ceilings and shooting people down. I prefer subtle. Let's say Ronald or your landlord comes here and gets hostile. If you have the white button pressed, the defense is monitoring the situation. Talking is fine. One of them puts a hand on you or pulls out a weapon, it will react."

I sort of thought that was cool, but what if Mel hugged me or something?

"Darts will fire, rendering them unconscious in a matter of seconds. In a situation where there is more than one person and it's more hostile, the defenses will be more severe. I wouldn't worry about that." He took a vial out of his pocket. "I retrieved your blood from the hospital, that's how I got your DNA."

I nodded in disbelief. "And what if someone touches me in a not hostile way? A hug or something?"

Lee smiled proudly. "That is a great question. If someone enters your home while the white button is engaged, just speak the words, '*Ally disengage.*' What that will do is only excuse the one person. However, if there's more than one person, you need to say, '*Party disengage.*' When the door shuts, it will stop assessing invited guests."

"Maybe I should write this down," I mumbled, and began to stand up to grab a piece of paper.

"No. It's not hard to remember. Never leave a vulnerability like that around. In the wrong hands, your own protection can become your worst enemy." He handed me the box. "Let's practice. I will step out. You hit the white button. I will go to attack you. Watch what happens."

"And what will I do when you're out cold on my floor from the snooze darts?"

Lee smirked. "I am prepared."

I watched him leave and as soon as the door shut, I opened the box and hit the white button.

"Engaged," a lovely female voice said. Fancy.

Lee knocked and I got up to answer the door. He stepped in, smiling, and waited until I shut the door. Neither of us spoke. He lifted his arms and went to strangle me. I flinched because that was just what I did these days, but it didn't deter Lee. He had just gotten his hand on my neck when I heard two whistle sounds as darts shot out from I didn't know where, hitting Lee in the arm, and would have hit his neck if he hadn't dropped to the ground.

"Go hit the white button again," Lee said as he laid on the floor, unmoving.

I did as he asked, then heard the female voice say, "Disengaged." As I ran back over to him, he was removing the dart from his arm.

"I wear a special material under my clothes. The darts can't penetrate. The darts will need to be replaced every week. I will come by and do that." I nodded as he stood. "Now, go hit the white button again and when you open the door, say, '*Ally disengage.*'"

I did as I was told and this time, it went way differently, as in nothing happened. A half an hour later, Lee was gathering his things and bidding me farewell. I thanked him, but he didn't acknowledge it.

I was in desperate need of a shower. I could still smell the hospital on me. I grabbed some clothes and went into the bathroom, glad there were no cameras in there.

The cast on my arm was removable. It wasn't for a broken arm, it was on because I'd sprained my wrist. Thank god, because

I had to work at Joker's Sin the next day and a cast would have Atlas showing me the door.

As I stood under the warm spray, I thought about Black. I was like gum on his shoe constantly. Suddenly, he gets wind that I was roughed up and he turned all terminator on me. Did he genuinely care or was he protecting his delivery boy? That was likely it. I ran all over the place delivering packages for Black. That was the agreement. When I had seen Mace and Bill kill a guy, I could've been next. Black saw something in me the day I had sat in his office. It was scary how he knew I wasn't going to say anything. There hadn't been too many deliveries, but they always needed to be dropped off way out of the way or in a weird place. I was sure there weren't a lot of people who want to do grunt work or would do it without questions. I wasn't the best choice, it was a lack of options sort of thing.

After my shower, I dressed in just pajama bottoms, brushed my teeth, and plopped on the couch. I didn't have much, but I had my PS4, music, and now a kickass security system. I never shut the white button off, so I knew it was all engaged.

It was weird knowing at any time, Black could turn on the monitors and watch me, but it also made me feel safer.

It all slipped away as I began to play awkwardly since my wrist was sore. It was well past one in the morning when I shut the TV down and went to bed. I took some pain meds for my headache that had gotten worse from playing video games, drank some water, and passed out.

Chapter Seven

Black

Jones, Lee, and I sat around a small table at Quirks and Perks the next morning. We all knew Quill wouldn't be working, but one thing Jones had found out as he researched Ronald Sterling was that he came here every morning for his coffee. My guess, it was where he had caught Quill's eye in the first place. I had no problem with how people met, who they fucked, or what made them happy, unless their happiness caused pain and suffering to another.

I made a lot of money inflicting pain and death. I made an equal amount protecting and securing. But nothing I or my people did was to undeserving people… mostly. Situations were weighed. Like in the instance where Bill and Mace had to draw Zagan out, innocent bystanders got killed. Some may argue it was avoidable. I'd tell them to shut the fuck up because they weren't in it making the hard calls.

"Where is this donkey fucker?" Jones asked as he pushed his empty mug across the table.

"Maybe part of the terms of his bail was to stay away from Quill. Did you not even research that?" Lee spoke to Jones in a way I had never heard. Usually, Lee was calm, collected, and supportive of everything that man did. Hell, he had risked life and limb over a year ago when Jones had been implicated as a mole in my organization. He was tortured in a chair by Bill over Jones. Now, he was snapping and acting like…

"Fuck you, Lee, don't get all dog ate my prime rib on me."

"What the hell does that even mean? No one says that," Lee

interrupted, and suddenly, I realized I was in the middle of a lover's quarrel.

"Knock it off," the woman behind the counter, Melissa, shouted. "This isn't Divorce Court, so take it outside."

Lee and Jones zipped their mouths. Lee was the only one who seemed embarrassed by his actions. Jones never gave a shit about what people thought.

The bells chiming above the café door had all three of us turning. There was no question that was Ronald Sterling. Even if I hadn't seen his picture, I'd know a dickless douchebag a mile away.

"Good morning, Melissa," Ronald said to the woman who looked like she was going to jump the counter and beat him to death with to-go cups.

"You're no longer allowed in here, Ronnie. As manager, I am banning you from Quirks and Perks. We have the right to refuse service. Now leave." She pointed to the door, her face red as a tomato. I had to give it to her, she was likely terrified, but she stood her ground.

"I'll have a French vanilla coffee, large, please." He slapped his credit card on the counter, completely ignoring Melissa's refusal of service.

"No. Get out or I'll call the cops."

"Don't bother," I said as I stood. I sauntered over, buttoning my jacket as I did. Ronald looked me up and down, and when I was only a foot from him, I experienced great joy when he had to look up to meet my eyes.

"Ronald Sterling, I've been waiting for you to arrive." I shot Melissa a wink, which only made her scowl. "I promise to escort Mr. Sterling out as soon as I'm done here."

I knew she wanted to say something, but when Lee and Jones joined me, she simply nodded and went back to doing whatever she had been doing before Ronald arrived.

"I don't know who you are, who any of you are, and I'm not going to sit here or anywhere with you." Ronald took a step back. "My father practically owns Haven Hart. I just have to say the word and Quirks and Perks crumbles. Or any of you do." He stood as tall as he could; it was adorable how he thought of himself as intimidating to me.

I took a moment to really look at him. He wasn't drop dead gorgeous, but there was a certain amount of appeal to his features. His suit was expensive and nicely put together. He overdid the cologne and I was getting tired of the scent. I noticed a lot of rich pricks all bought the same one.

He wasn't taller or bigger than I was. But he wasn't tiny, either. I could tell he had some muscles under his designer suit and there was no doubt, to Quill, Ronald Sterling was evil.

"I'm not asking you, Mr. Sterling, I'm demanding you sit with me. And I dare say, Mr. Hart would love it if your dear father told him that he owned his town." Jones and Lee took the opportunity to stand behind Ronald. I was glad there wasn't a lot of people here, and those that were, weren't paying much attention. "I'd also like to add that any power your father may have isn't yours. So shut up, sit down, and listen to what I have to say. Then when I'm done, you can fuck right off out that door, which I encourage you to do, and never come back."

Ronald opened his mouth to speak, but the nudge Jones gave him shut him up. We decided to take the far booth in the back, away from the few patrons that were here. Jones pushed Ronald into the booth and quickly sat beside him so he couldn't bolt. Lee sat across from him, and I was on the end. It was a perfect set up.

"I don't know who you are or why I'm being treated this way. Like you said, my father's power is his own, not mine. So if he's angered you, take it up with him." Ronald's eyes darted between the three of us, and the fine sheen of sweat across his forehead confirmed his nervousness.

"This has nothing to do with your father and everything to do with you and your actions against one of my men." Even though Quill only did deliveries, just like with the landlord, putting Quill under my umbrella of protection worked well.

"I just said I didn't know you, how the hell—" Ronald didn't get further in his sentence. Jones smacked him so hard in the back of the head, he almost slammed his nose against the table.

"Respect," Jones demanded in his gravely timbre.

"How about you shut your mouth for a minute and hear what Mr. Black is trying to tell you?" Lee said softly but firmly.

When Ronald just nodded, I continued. "Quill Almeida." I let the name hang in the air for a minute. When Ronald's eyes widened, I expected him to be terrified, but instead, he looked livid.

"That little punk ass—" Again, Jones hit him.

"I'll do this all day if I have to." Jones chuckled darkly.

"Quill Almeida works for me and whatever the two of you had at one point is over. This isn't a question, Mr. Sterling, it's an order. Maybe in your case, a warning. I didn't enjoy taking him home from the hospital after you went a few rounds on him." I reached into my jacket pocket, amused when Ronald flinched, likely thinking I was about to take out a gun. Instead, I took out a business card and slid it over to him.

"Red Rose Securities?" He flipped it over, and I knew what he was reading there. My name. Black didn't hold water for people like the Sterlings. Terrance Blackrose did, however. "You own Red Rose Securities?"

"I do. So you understand my reach, Mr. Sterling. Now, I don't want to have to bring this to your father, but I will. Quill will be pressing charges. You will take whatever punishment is dealt to you." As best I could, I leaned across the table. "If it were up to me, you'd be laying in an alleyway with a bullet between your eyes. But that's not how this works and I dare say, Quill wouldn't like that." I didn't honestly care what Quill thought if I decided to do that, but in this instance, I wanted Ronald to think Quill mattered to me and my business. What better way to do that than to make power hungry fools think someone else had power over them.

Ronald was silent for a few seconds before Jones smacked him in the back of the head again.

"Have you gone stupid?" Jones asked.

"No." Ronald rubbed the back of his head, only causing Jones to laugh. "I get it." He looked at me with a flicker of determination. "What makes you think Quill will press charges?" He scoffed, "He wouldn't press charges against his brother or his last two exes, and they weren't half as powerful as my family. I think you don't know your guy as well as you think you do."

This time when Jones went to hit him, he ducked.

"This is your one and only warning. You let me deal with Quill. Maybe it's you who doesn't know him very well." I wouldn't let on that Ronald's words had upset me. Who were all these people in Quill's life that felt like he was a punching bag and why had he done nothing about it?

I had no love for the authorities, but I had my own reasons for that. I couldn't help as the curiosity that was Quill began to niggle at my mind.

This conversation was over, so I got out and began walking toward the door. Jones and Lee made sure Ronald followed right behind me.

"You never step foot in there again," I said as my car drove up to the curb.

Ronald didn't say anything further, just walked toward what I assumed was his Mustang.

"You want me watching him?" Jones asked.

"Absolutely." I got in my car and as it drove off, I was on the phone with Lana, asking her to make arrangements for Quill to meet me in the office the next morning.

Chapter Eight

Quill

As I got ready for work at Joker's Sin, I kept the removable cast on. My wrist was sore and I couldn't take a lot of the pain killers since I had to be sharp to work. I would remove the cast when I got to work and stick it in my locker. With make-up, I'd try to cover as much of the bruising as I could.

Each night, Atlas, my boss at the club, had something different going on. With so many clubs popping up around the city, he had to constantly compete with them to stay new and fresh. Tonight was leather night. Normally, I'd fuss that I had nothing to wear or that I couldn't afford it. Atlas was good about that stuff and always had something on hand for his ideas and for his guys to wear. I happened to own a red leather outfit. I say outfit lightly. It consisted of red leather pants, a red vest, and bitching boots with a reasonable heel. I was allowed to wear my black bracelets, and tattoos weren't a problem if anyone had any. I put all my piercings back in that the hospital had made me remove. I didn't always wear them all, but having them on felt like a special layer of protection. I'd had them all for so many years, they didn't close up on me and if they started to, pushing through the weak skin was no big deal for me. Atlas never cared how we represented ourselves as long as we weren't adorned in Nazi tattoos or anything racist.

I went with my red contacts, and my black hair was working for me right now. I was thinking of coloring it teal tomorrow. I shrugged at my internal debate.

It was winter, so there was no way I was walking to the bus

stop dressed like this. All I owned was a black puff jacket Melissa had bought me when she saw me walking home in a hoodie last year... in February. I grabbed the coat and wrapped myself snug inside. The hood protected my ears from the winter air and would simply have to do.

I hadn't disengaged the security in my apartment and knew it wasn't hostile toward me, so I left my apartment with it engaged, feeling slightly better that no one would be waiting for me inside my place when I stumbled in at around three in the morning.

As I walked to the bus stop, I checked my voicemail. I'd decided to ignore my phone for the day in favor of sleeping and playing video games. There was one from Mel saying she loved me and that there were visitors at the coffee shop today and to call her later and she'd tell me all about it. Another was from Lana, Black's secretary, telling me he expected me in his office tomorrow morning at around nine. Awesome, sleeping in wasn't going to happen now.

I just stepped on the bus as my call to Mel went through.

"Hey," she said, sounding exhausted. "How you feeling?"

"I'm fine. On the bus."

I heard her release a sigh and knew she wanted to fight with me on not taking a few days off. But I had bills to pay, another hospital one too, and I always needed some cushion in case my brother came back.

"So, tell me about these visitors you had today. Sounds exciting." I had fifteen minutes or so before my stop and Mel didn't babble, so I knew I'd get the full story by the time I arrived.

"Your Thor was here with two of his guys for like an hour. I couldn't figure out why, because Black doesn't come in often. He usually has someone get coffee for him or he is in and out fast. But when Ronnie arrived, it became clear why he was there."

Why was Black doing all this? Why the hell did he care?
"What happened, Mel?"

"The three sat there and when Ronnie came in, I was trying to kick him out but he was all, I'm me and you're you, blah blah blah—"

"Mel, why would you do that? Just let him buy his coffee and go. He's a Sterling!" My voice rose, causing a couple of people to turn toward me.

"I'm not afraid of him or them, Quill."

I knew that wasn't true, but I didn't want to fight with her. "Then what happened?"

"Oh my god," she chuckled. "You should have seen it. They took Ronnie into a booth. One guy kept hitting him in the back of the head. When it was over, they all left and Ronnie practically ran to his car."

Fucking Christ. "Shit. Doesn't Black realize all he's managed to do is make my life worse by getting involved?"

"Quill." She whispered, "Maybe your life was hard because no one ever did step in. Ever think of that?"

The bus was pulling up to my stop, so I had to end the call with Mel. I promised I'd call her tomorrow. Speaking of tomorrow, no wonder Black wanted to see me in his office.

Even though I was able to get make-up on my face and put kohl around my eyes, Atlas saw all. One look at me and he knew I wasn't at my best.

"Damn, Kid, why you here if you're still recovering?" he asked as he pulled me into his office.

"I need the money. Please don't send me home. I can work."

He shook his head, but told me to get behind the bar with Max. I was to help him out, but no heavy lifting. Whatever, I was just glad to be getting paid.

The place was filled with leather-clad hotties. Some were creative with their outfits, hoping to win the grand prize of a lap dance from Atlas and a free night of drinks.

About two hours into work, Max said he had to take a break

for ten to use the bathroom. I had about five other bartenders working the circular bar that surrounded the stage. I told him I could do it on my own for ten minutes, and he left.

I loved how even though my body ached, my head pounded, and I wasn't looking my best, I was able to still get a few numbers tossed my way. Made a person feel good.

"Excuse me," someone shouted. I turned with a smile to help the patron.

"Hey, how can I—" I stopped midsentence as Ronnie stood on the other side of the bar. Even though I knew I wasn't in any danger with the bar between us, the fear was permanent.

"How can you help me?" he sneered. "You have your boss come and embarrass me in public? Threaten me? You can help by taking a break, meeting me in the back, and begging me to forgive you."

That wasn't going to happen. "I'm not doing that, Ronnie. Even if I wanted to, and I don't, Max just took a break. I can't leave."

"You are nothing but a lowlife whore, Quill. Fucking your way to the top. It's all you'll ever be," he yelled over the loud music. A few people were paying attention to the obvious argument. "Maybe I should drop a line to your brother and let him know where he can find you. Heard he's been looking for you for a few months now. Bet you'd get down on your knees and beg me to forgive you if I kept your whereabouts quiet, huh?"

Dylan Almeida was a nightmare. Made Ronnie look like a Care Bear. The second I was able to get away from him and my shit family, I did. Unfortunately, I couldn't get far enough. I went back to Haven Hart where I was born, hoping I'd be safe. Dylan found me a year ago, and by the time he left, he made sure I knew that if he ever saw me again and I had nothing to offer, he'd kill me. Whenever Dylan found me, I always packed up and moved on. In this case, I hadn't. I loved Haven Hart, and I hoped

Dylan would assume I'd moved on and wouldn't think of returning here.

"Ronnie, if I'm all those things, why would you want to be with me in the first place?"

I saw Max return, but he just went to the waiting patrons, never snapping at me to get back to work.

"It's the principal of it all, Quill. Your boss said you're pressing charges against me. I really think you should reconsider that. With all I know about you and about why you're running from your brother, it would be wise for you to let those charges drop. Got me?" He threw some cash in my face and walked away. I couldn't see where as the crowd swallowed him up.

What the fuck has Black done to me?

Chapter Nine

Black

It felt like I had just closed my eyes when the sound of my cell going off woke me. Who the fuck was calling me now? The clock read twelve. I didn't often get to bed early, this was the first night in a long time. Clearly, the powers that be didn't like that idea.

Jones' name glowed on the screen. "Yeah."

"I woke you." Jones didn't apologize, just stated a fact.

"You're a fucking genius, Jones. What other tricks are you going to pull out of your sleeve?" I had no time for this shit. I wanted to get back to my amazing dream.

"I was tracking Ronnie like you asked. Followed him to Joker's Sin. Didn't think much about it, except none of you told me Quill worked there. That information would have been nice, boss." I knew Jones hated surprises.

"Shit. What happened?"

"Ronnie is currently sitting at a table, watching Quill's every move. He went up to get a drink, they had words, and by the look on your boy's face, it wasn't anything good."

My boy's face? What the fuck? "He's not my boy. Keep eyes on him, I'm on my way. We got anyone free right now?"

There was a lot of sound, so I knew Jones was moving deeper into the club. He'd stay completely hidden. Ronnie wouldn't know he was ever there.

"Everyone's out on jobs. The new guys, you haven't cleared them yet."

My own demons were holding me back on okaying anyone

43

else. What Emma did, infiltrating my organization and practically destroying it, had hit me hard. I had to adjust.

"Call Ginger. I want him to locate the whereabouts of Bartholomew Sterling. Then I want him in my office in the morning at nine." Ginger was the best of the new recruits. A wisp of a thing, but he shocked us all in his testing. Especially Jones.

"Ginger? You sure he's ready?"

"I'm not repeating my orders, Jones. I'm almost dressed. Make sure Quill stays safe."

Tossing my phone on the bed, I grabbed a pair of black jeans and a white, long-sleeved shirt. I didn't have time to braid my hair, so I brushed it quickly. It felt uncomfortable not wearing a suit, but I'd stick out too much at Joker's Sin in a three piece suit. Placing my phone in my pocket, I opted not to call my driver and instead went down to the garage. My Charger sat beautiful and black, and as I slipped into the leather seats and started her up, I couldn't help but smile at the familiar vibration as I revved the engine.

I parked my car as close to Joker's Sin as I could. I took my leather jacket off the seat and quickly put it on, hit the alarm, and made my way toward the club. There was still a line after midnight. The place closed in two hours, why would people wait that long? Well, I wasn't.

"Can I help you?" the large bouncer asked.

"No." I barreled through him and made my way into the club. It was like dubstep nation in there and so much fucking leather.

"Hey." I felt someone tap my shoulder. I whipped around and grabbed whomever it was by the neck. It was the bouncer from the door.

"Not today, Junior. You tell Atlas, Black is here. Now fuck off." I pushed him away and made my way to the bar. I hadn't been inside Joker's Sin before, I only knew how it looked based on Mace and Bill's description.

I liked the concept and would've taken more time to appreciate it if I wasn't hell-bent on finding Quill.

"Can I help you, handsome?" I turned and looked down. A small guy with pink hair and barely-there black leather shorts had spoken.

"No. Where's Quill?"

The small man slid his fingers down my arm. "Mmm. Quill didn't tell me he had a God for a boyfriend. You're better than most I see him with." He jerked his head to the right. I followed the direction and there before me, was Quill.

He was dressed in red leather. I couldn't see below the waist, but the vest he wore was tight against his pale skin. I knew he loved his bracelets, and he had them all on tonight. His arms were covered in red and silver glitter, making him stick out like a gorgeous disco ball. It looked like he had put all of his piercings back in, and I could see when the light shown on his face, he also had glitter on his cheeks.

"I'll just leave you to it," the small man said with a chuckle, and I took the few steps to where Quill stood mixing drinks.

He hadn't noticed me yet, and I got a chance to see he had red eyes and black liner on his lids. He looked like pure sin. I was surprised when I felt my cock stiffen. Until now, I was never sexually interested in Quill. Okay, to be fair, I admired him. He was stunning, but there was a line cut somewhere between admiration and want. Why was I feeling something now?

"Are you following me?" Quill's voice snapped me back to attention.

"I thought you wanted me to follow you."

Quill narrowed his eyes, but I saw how he swallowed as he took me in. He was a flirt by nature and no matter how peeved he was at me, he could never sustain that anger.

"Your hair is down. And you're not in a suit... And," he reached out, lightly fingered a strand of my hair, "it's like silk."

"I use a very special treatment." I didn't really understand why I was having this conversation. I wanted to tell Quill he had to go back home where the security system would keep him safe, but there he was, flirting, but something about him seemed different to me.

"Hmm. I like it. What's it smell like?" He leaned forward, and I actually found myself meeting him so he could sniff my fucking hair when I felt another hand on my shoulder. *What was with these touchy people?*

"Who the fuck do you think you are?" I knew Ronald Sterling's voice. With my back to him and my hair down, he likely had no idea who I was. He also didn't know I wasn't alone. This time, I wasn't in the middle of a coffee shop and I'd had enough.

Watching Quill's body lock up and the sheer fear that transformed his smiling face into a terrified one pissed me off. I knew Ronald was on my left and my size had pushed people away. I spun, fist ready, and made a connection with his face that was quite satisfying. He fell back a good foot, taking dancing people down with him.

"Goddammit, Black!" Atlas stood between me and Ronald, who lay bleeding on the floor.

I didn't pay Atlas any mind at all. I took a couple steps and hovered over Ronnie's body. "I warned you. That was a courtesy."

"You don't own this town," Ronnie shouted, spraying blood with his spit. "Quill hasn't told me to leave him alone."

Knowing Jones was close, I turned my back on Ronnie. Atlas was ordering his men to help Ronnie up and clean the mess. My eyes locked with Quill's red ones.

"That right?" I asked him. "You want him?"

Quill's gaze darted from me to Ronnie. So much fear, so much anger. He was on a precipice. I couldn't help him make this call. But if Quill said he wanted Ronnie, I knew I'd have little choice.

He shook his head and I wanted to hug him for being so brave. "I... I don't want him, Black. I told him to leave me alone."

That was all I needed to hear. I spun around. Ronnie was upright now, aided by two bouncers I chose to ignore. Gripping his shirt, I pulled him closer to me.

"Now you've heard it. I see you near him, you will lose your eye sight. You talk to him, you will lose your tongue. You touch him, I will take your hands... Do you see where I'm going with this? I will kill you in inches, Mr. Sterling."

"My father will hear about this." Ronnie's voice shook, but he wasn't backing down how I'd hoped. He was either a fucking idiot or he had far too much faith in his father.

"Oh, I'm counting on it."

The bouncers escorted Ronnie out of the club and when they went to grab me, Atlas intervened. "Not him. He's going to my office."

I didn't miss the glare Atlas gave Quill as we passed, and I was sure Quill wanted to follow me into that office with Atlas. But it was better this way. I knew Jones was still lurking, but he was going to follow Ronnie and note where he went. Quill was fine behind the bar for now.

Inside Atlas' office, I explained as best I could why I was there. When I told him Quill was an employee of mine and that when harm came to my people, I intervened, there were a lot more questions thrown my way. I couldn't answer them, nor would I.

"I don't much like you and your people, Black," Atlas said as he drank down his whiskey. His dark skin made the white leather outfit he wore practically glow. He was a stunning man with his long braids, flawless skin, and sculpted body. "You cause me a lot of grief. First Mace and Bill, now you—"

"You hold on a minute there, Atlas. You're alive because of

my people. You are the one who got in bed with a psychopath. If my guys hadn't shook the hornets' nest when they did, I am sure Zagan Marks would have you buried so deep, you'd be as gone as Hoffa." I couldn't sit there anymore. I got up, adjusted my jacket, and made for the door.

"Is Quill going to bring more trouble to my club?"

I gripped the handle, angry enough to crush it if I wanted. A part of me wanted to say yes and he should fire him. Another part knew as much as I wanted to do that, Quill would hate it. I was having a hard time swallowing that pill, and the why of it was irritating.

"He will have someone with him at all times until this situation is resolved. He's not a danger to you or this place."

Without listening to what Atlas had to say after that, I left. Quill was still working the bar, smiling once more. I stepped up in time to hear the pink-haired guy from earlier say something to Quill.

"Your boyfriend is intense, Quill."

Quill shrugged, his smile dimming. "He's not mine. No way would someone like him touch someone like me. But I have fun flirting."

Even though Quill and I couldn't be, I didn't understand why he thought he couldn't get a decent human being to be with.

"Well, I might try then," pink dude said as he pointed over Quill's shoulder, which had me face to face with red, nervous eyes.

"Be my guest," Quill answered, but I knew he didn't mean that. It was easy to read him. He either didn't know how to lie or gave up trying a long time ago.

"I was just on my way out," I answered. "Quill, you're off at two thirty. A car will take you home and I will see you in my office at nine. Have a nice evening, boys."

The widening of Quill's eyes and the pink that covered his

cheeks told me if I didn't get out of there now, there'd be another scene. So as quickly as I could, I left.

I read my texts on the way to my car. Jones said he followed Ronnie back to his place and it looked like the guy was calling it a night. I arranged a car to meet Quill at two thirty and take him home. I hoped Quill wouldn't give my driver a hard time, but I made it clear to my driver it was a non-negotiable ride.

I was sure I'd hear all about why I was an asshole in the morning, and I strangely looked forward to it.

Chapter Ten

Quill

I didn't give Black's driver a hard time when he greeted me at the end of my shift. I got in the car, leaned my head against the cool glass, and as the world passed by, I replayed the entire evening in my head.

Black flirted with me, he punched a guy, and not just any guy: Ronald Sterling. Black was a God among men, in my opinion, so I supposed seeing him knock Ronnie down shouldn't have shocked me and had fear trickling through my veins like poison. I didn't know why Black was doing any of this.

When his silver eyes met mine and asked me if I wanted Ronnie, every ounce of me wanted to shout, "*No, I want you.*" But I couldn't, so I did the next best thing. I said I didn't want Ronnie. Knowing that if Black ever turned his back on me, I'd be screwed. I didn't feel brave a lot of the time, but something about Black's presence made me feel on top of the world.

Before it had all gone to shit, when Black leaned against the bar and let me touch his golden hair, there was a twinkle of playful mischief in his beautiful eyes and, for a second, I pretended he was my boyfriend visiting me at work. But Ronnie had come in like a splash of cold water on my life. It was always something with me. I wasn't destined for a happily ever after.

Black's driver stayed until I was securely in the building before driving off. Inside my apartment was like being in a bubble of contentment. I knew Black could watch me at any time, but I also knew it wasn't his style.

As I stripped the red leather from my body, I let myself wonder why I surrounded myself with dangerous people. If I had learned anything these last few months, it was how there were levels to the evil. I knew Black killed people. I was aware what his organization was all about.

Under the spray of my shower, I replayed that night in his office when he'd called me over a few months back.

"When I give people chances, I only ever give them one, Quill. Me letting you live is the only chance you'll get." Black sat back against his office chair, staring at me through silver slits.

"Wait a sec, I blew my one chance because I was taking out the trash and your guys were stupid enough to shoot a man in an alley where I work? Am I hearing you right?" I felt bold in front of this man... I also felt very horny.

"You got a mouth on you."

"You got a while, I'll show you exactly what this mouth can do." Flirting, I could do, and if it kept me alive, I'd do anything.

"You're not whoring yourself out to me. Besides, you're less than half my age. I don't rob the cradle." Black chuckled around the rim of his whiskey glass.

"I've probably seen more than most people you know. God knows I've walked, built a home, and planted roots in Hell." I needed to shut up.

The silence was unnerving. For a large man, Black moved with a muted grace. He stood, his height forcing me to look up, and slowly stalked over to me. I felt his footsteps like a pulse.

"What do you know about what I do?" When he was so close I could smell him, he leaned down, resting his hands on the arms of the chair I was shaking in.

"Um... I'm going to guess, okay?" He nodded. "Right, so, I'd like to say model, because you're gorgeous. But by your scowl, I will say I'm wrong.... Let's go with a really fucking nice guy who lets silly boys who do their jobs go free?"

Black hung his head and I couldn't help but inhale. Damn it, his scent was doing things to me.

51

"Is everything a joke to you?" Black asked as his eyes met mine.

"It has to be."

Black furrowed his brow and I felt my cheeks burn with his scrutiny. "Why?"

Lying was my go-to, even if I was only half good at it, but with Black this close, I couldn't find my filter. "Because if I let reality in all the time, I won't much want to live in this world. Would you?"

It was in that moment, I saw he really did understand. He lived in the same Hell I did. And when he spoke, I wasn't sure if I was glad or terrified.

"I run an assassin organization. My security company masks that. You want to live, then you work for me."

Work for him? "Yeah, I'm a lover, not a fighter."

He stood and walked back to his desk. "I don't want you to kill anyone, Quill. I need a delivery boy. Someone who won't ask questions. Won't look at what he's carrying and just do what he's told. Can I count on you to be that person?"

Can I count on you? I couldn't remember the last time anyone asked me that.

"Yes."

When the water began to chill, I shut it off and grabbed a towel. That night in Black's office had changed my whole life. I felt important, needed. People in my life, sans Mel, made me feel like I was just existing. I wasn't vital to the everyday of things. Often, they said exactly that. I wasn't worth it. I was a waste. A whore. I was on this earth as a step stool for those greater. I had heard it all. Black was the first to actually see me, really see.

Flirting with him was who I was, but if I was being honest, I wanted that man more than I ever wanted anything. When Ronnie beat me up and I never showed for that package, knowing I had disappointed him was worse than any punch.

I was sure he was amused by me at the club, but in my heart, I knew he'd likely never be with me how I wanted to be with him.

After I dried off and brushed my teeth, I slid under my covers and stared at the ceiling. I wondered what Black would say in the morning. How much shit was I in now?

Sleep claimed me eventually, and I dreamed of what Black's smile would look like when directed at me. What his laughter sounded like when I told a cheesy joke. I dreamed of lazy Sundays, manic Mondays, and a life time of no pain, just love.

Chapter Eleven

Black

It was a quarter to nine, and I sat in my office with Ginger, Jones, Lee, and Lana. Quill still had fifteen minutes, so I wasn't pissed yet. Lee was by the window, his laptop open on the small glass table. Every so often, his eyes would lift and he watched Ginger and Jones, who were having a quiet conversation on my leather couch.

For the last year, Ginger had been put through some rigorous tests. Mace had found him pickpocketing on the streets, and he was really good according to Mace. At one point, he got caught and was able to knock the guy out with a jab to the side of his head and was gone before anyone knew who he was.

I'd offered Ginger the same offer I did to all of my people. Work for me and thrive. Don't, and maybe someone finds out about you. It wasn't the best tactic, but I'd built some amazingly loyal people from that proposal. I knew their passions and where they would fit in my organization. Ginger was quick, fast, and surprisingly lethal. The fact he was brilliant was a plus.

Looking at him, you wouldn't think he was an assassin, and that was the best kind of killer. He had a shock of red hair, styled but short, and sometimes I saw him with glasses, but not always. His cinnamon freckles were almost as adorable as his childlike smile he gave most people. He was small and thin. Reminded me of Quill in that respect. Ginger loved his retro t-shirts with odd sayings or 80's movie logos. He seemed to like music he deemed oldie, but made me wince thinking he thought Debbie Gibson was in that genre. He looked more like a geeky college student than a genius assassin.

Jones and he hit it off right away, and wasn't that odd. Jones hated most everyone except Lee. Lee, who was giving those two a glare that screamed death. Not sure what was up there, but I made a note to talk with Lee later.

"He's here," Lana said as she put her phone away. The desk in the lobby always informed us when people were heading up. "I'll meet him at the elevators and bring him here."

"Thank you." Once Lana left, I called Ginger's name. "I'm going to be doing the talking here. Only speak when I tell you to. Quill is rattled enough, and I need him calm."

"Sure thing," Ginger said with a stupid smile.

"I just don't think peach is the right color for you, Lana, especially in winter. Pastels are perfect in spring and summer. If you start wearing them now, people will be like, 'oh, there's Lana, the yearly Easter egg.' You will kill a royal blue or dark red. Especially with that black hair of yours," Quill said animatedly to Lana as he entered my office. She was hanging on his every word and… was she taking notes?

"Quill," I said, interrupting their fashion conversation. He looked up, eyes wide as he surveyed the room filled with people. All but one he knew. "This is Ginger, he works for me. Have a seat."

"Hey, Ginger, is that because of the hair or do you kill people with spice?" Quill winked and snapped, and while it was clever, I had no time for this.

"Um…" Ginger was at a loss, and wasn't that typical Quill.

"We need to talk," I stated, saving Ginger.

"Right." Quill took a seat next to the couch but far enough from everyone. I noticed the only thing at his back was the bar, and he could see the whole room. That said more about Quill than many would observe.

"Ginger, here, did some work for me last night. I was looking for Bartholomew Sterling, Ronald's father."

"Why would you do that?" Quill snapped. "Leave it alone. Haven't you caused me enough shit?" He quickly covered his mouth like he realized who he was talking to a little late.

"One, you don't tell me what to do. Two, what I've done is help you climb out of the shithole you fell into. Three, I'm not sitting here asking you, I am telling you. You work for me. Ronald is interfering in my business. Having you laid up in a hospital room hindered a package getting where it had to go. Thank God, Lee was available. I make promises to very powerful people and the reason they come back time and time again is because I do not break them." I recognized my voice was beginning to rise, something I tried very hard to keep in check. Quill had this way of enhancing all my emotions.

"I see," Quill whispered. "It's because my being in the hospital almost made you break a promise." He closed his eyes for the briefest moment, and the sadness in his color-of-the-day brown eyes was prominent.

"What did you think this was about?" Jones scoffed.

"I didn't ask to hear from you." I shot a finger at Jones. "Let's move on from this. Now, Quill, I wanted to talk to you after a conversation I had with Ronald at Quirks and Perks yesterday morning…"

"I know about it." Quill sounded like a moody teenager, and if that didn't shine a light on our age gap, nothing did.

"From the way my run in with him just went, I'm sure you're smart enough to figure out that things are strained. I had hoped he got the message originally, but it's quite clear he's either obsessed with you or hates losing." I watched Quill as I spoke, his face giving nothing away. He seemed bored.

"Ginger is going to tell us about what he found out about Bartholomew Sterling, and then I need to talk to you alone." That got a reaction out of Quill, just a quirk of his lips. "Ginger?"

"Right. I was surprised to find Daddy Sterling had his itinerary on his website, so if you want him dead, it won't be hard." His nonchalant attitude reminded me so much of Jones, and when said man chuckled, I realized he must have thought the same thing. "Anyway. He's not a perfect human being. Slimy, sort of, but he gives a lot to charity, and as I watched him in public at some gathering, he was charming his way through the crowd. I couldn't stay long as I only got a few hours there. It was late when Jones told me to scope him out." He scrolled on his phone. "He is going to a charity event tomorrow night at The Camille Hotel."

Quill sat in his seat, rolling his eyes as Ginger spoke, and I had to interrupt Ginger to ask what his encounters with the father had been like.

"He's a cocky asshole. Ronnie doesn't have Bart's finesse, but he's just as awful as his son. Ronnie is the bull in the china shop, Bart's the mouse." Quill began picking at a white thread on his jeans. "I only met him a couple times." The last sentence was a garble of words, but I made them out.

"Do you think he's aware of what his son is about?" I asked, and Quill chuckled.

"He raised him. Of course, he knows."

I scanned the room, taking in everyone's faces. All likely thinking what I was. *What would make father turn against son?*

"Quill, you said Ronnie was a bull and his father was a mouse. Explain that," Lee asked from his table by the window.

He shrugged. "Both cause as much damage; one is just sneakier than the other. Ronnie is open in his shittiness. Bart isn't, he will nibble the cables. Ronnie tears through the electronics, you get me?"

"And would you say Ronnie's public behavior would be angering to his father?" Lana asked, her eyes full of sorrow for Quill.

"Oh no," Quill jolted up. "You're going to try to turn them on each other? You high?"

"Something tells me Ronnie is only scared of one person, his father. I will do what I have to, to get rid of Ronnie. I would rather not kill him, just because it wouldn't be good for business." It wouldn't be. Bartholomew was a saint in this town. Only because the people didn't know the real him. So many wouldn't stop until they found the monsters who killed his son. I didn't need that kind of heat on me right now. That didn't mean I wouldn't if I couldn't get Ronnie to back down. I'd killed many powerful figures, but they weren't living in my town. It would be a challenge.

"Okay." Quill's tone was sarcastic. "I'll just give Lana my info so you can order my tombstone now. If you wait a little and let me die on my birthday, you'll save yourself some money."

"So dramatic," Jones grumbled.

"No!" Quill shouted. "You have no idea what you're doing. Yeah, you kill the big baddies of the world, but did you ever stop and think about what Ronnie might do when backed against a wall? No, you didn't. He may never touch me again, hell, he may even leave me alone, but he will watch me suffer."

"Calm down, Quill." Lana got up, walked over to him, and gently hugged him. "No one is going to hurt you anymore." Her sharp gaze met mine over his shoulder. "Ever." She was making him a promise I had to keep.

"Oh Lana," Quill pulled back and kissed her forehead. "I like you. But you don't understand what he can do to me."

"Tell us, please?" she pleaded, but Quill just smiled softly and sat back down.

"I need you all to leave Quill and I alone," I directed, never taking my eyes off him. Through my periphery, I saw them all go. Lana left last, closing the door quietly.

Quill sat, shoulders slumped, and the rest of him proved he

was shattered. I had taken down bigger giants than the Sterlings. I knew people better than anyone else in the world. Quill wasn't afraid of the Sterlings. Ronnie and the pain didn't scare him. It was whatever knowledge Ronnie and his family harbored. I got up, the squeak of my chair making Quill flinch.

I sat on the couch Jones had vacated, as close to Quill as I could. His eyes were downcast, staring at his lap. He wasn't crying, yet the despair was there.

"I need you to tell me everything, Quill. I can't protect you if you don't."

He lifted his head and his eyes were like fire. "Protect me?" His laugh was humorless. "I never asked you to protect me. You've condemned me, Black."

"To what?" My fingers itched to grab and shake him into telling me what he had locked up inside.

"The only thing that has the power to gut you like no other…" His sparkle seemed so dim as he whispered, "Family."

Chapter Twelve

Quill

I couldn't believe I even told Black that much. It was just one word, but the heaviness and power of it was immense.

"Your family?" Black spoke so softly, like he thought I was going to bolt, and I really wanted to. I wanted to find a hole and crawl inside it.

"Can we not do this, Black? Can't I just be flighty Quill who ravishes you with my eyes, makes you horny with my words, and drives you batty?" I wanted off this topic badly.

"What makes you think you make me horny and... No, don't deflect." He shook a finger at me and I was glad to at least see his lips curl up. "You're good at that."

"You're a harder nut to crack than most thought." Sitting back, I regarded Black with the same uncertainty he seemed to show me. "I don't want to talk about my family, my past, or my life. Just know Ronnie has the knowledge that would open the gates, so to speak."

The flare of Black's nostrils braced me for his response. "I get pasts, we all have them, and most aren't pretty. But in order to keep you safe, I need to know what I'm fighting."

And that was the thing, his need to save me. "You don't need to protect me. Just let Ronnie be. He will leave me alone soon enough. Every time you or your guys ruffle his feathers, you start the cycle all over again."

While Black was all force and bending of the wills, he was generally in control of his temper. So when he kicked the table in front of him, sending it flying and crashing against the wall, I was taken aback. On reflex, I covered my head and huddled into a ball on the chair.

"Small target, be a small target," I whispered to myself.

When no one came running in, I feared I was about to get hit. Why would they run in to save me from Black? He was their boss, I was nobody.

But no blow came. No screaming or hair pulling, no degradation.

"Quill." I felt the air of his words against my arm that was securely covering my head. His voice was low, coaxing. "I'm not going to hurt you."

I'd heard that before many times, and the second I let my guard down, that was when they struck. I wasn't an idiot. I stayed in my ball; protected, safe.

"What did you do?" I heard Lana's voice, but I refused to look up.

"I got angry. I didn't touch him. I'd never do that." Black's voice was almost a plea.

"Of course, you wouldn't," Lana said, and I felt hands on my arm. "Sweetheart, it's Lana, can you look at me?"

Slowly, I peeked out, seeing only Lana's face. Her eyes brimmed with tears. It was quiet and as I peered around the room, I saw Black's back to me. He was looking out the window. His arms were wrapped around himself and he was taking big breaths. Lee, Jones, and Ginger were cleaning up the mess. Only Lana was paying attention to me.

"There you are." She smiled. "Black's bark is bigger than his bite. Please don't be afraid of him."

"I'd like to go home now." I said it so only Lana would hear, but apparently, Black had impeccable hearing.

"Quill, I'm sorry I reacted how I did. It's just… Look, I can't explain it, but you can't just give up on this. You can't let Ronnie win just because he has information. You can fight back and I will help you."

"Why?" I untangled myself, glad when Lana stayed close. "I'm just a delivery boy. I won't mess up again. I will deliver every package no matter what."

Black furrowed his brow, his expression that of disgust. "Is that what you think this is about? My deliveries?"

"Why else would you care?"

When his face began to turn red, I feared another outburst and hid behind Lana. Not my proudest moment.

"Jesus, Quill, stop cowering. I'm not going to hurt you. I'd do this for any of my guys." He took a step toward me, but stopped when a whimper escaped me.

"You didn't help Bill and Mace." I hadn't meant for that to slip out. I'd heard that Bill had called Black for help when he and Mace were stuck in the school at the hands of Zagan Marks. Mace lost a finger and was now scarred. Black never got there in time. He was supposed to be watching, and he never came.

"You don't understand that situation, Quill. Don't judge me for that."

"You have cameras in my place, watching me. If I need help, are you going to be too busy for me?" The terror began to subside and in the company of the others, I let anger take over. "I don't judge you, Black. I don't judge anyone. I just want to live my life one day at a time and maybe, not always patting myself on the back for surviving it, but be proud because I lived it."

Black shook his head, his gaze locked on mine. "You don't know me, Quill. You don't know how hard some of the decisions I have to make are. I can't be everywhere, you're right. Sometimes, I am too late. I knew Bill and Mace could get through that. I won't say more to you about it because it isn't your business." He took another few steps toward me. This time, I didn't back away. My mind knew I was safe.

"You need to understand something, Quill, I want you to survive your life so you can live it. That is why I have to protect you."

There was a time when Black questioned killing me. I knew he knew that. While I didn't know anything about his life or his family, I got a sense that his people were his family.

"I don't mean to interrupt," Jones said. "But I have a way you can make Bartholomew aware that Quill is off limits without tearing his face off."

"Yeah, it was all his idea, sure," Lee mumbled.

"Does whose idea it was really matter?" Jones snapped at Lee, and it was like being in the middle of a couple fighting. There was a vibe to it.

"Both of you better work out your shit before we meet again. I am not dealing with this." Black held two fingers up and pointed at both of them. "Now, what's your idea?"

Jones eyed Lee one last time before he spoke. "Go to the charity ball with Quill."

"What?" Black and I both said at the same time.

"Hear me out." Jones grabbed something off the printer and held it out for Black. "It's a charity for LGBT youth in Haven Hart. Mr. Hart has it every year even though he has yet to ever be seen at one. Anyone who's anyone wants to go in the hopes they will meet the elusive man."

"I don't have an invitation," Black said as he handed me the paper. It was an online article talking about it being the tenth year for Rainbow Hart Charity Ball for LGBT Youth.

Lee smiled like the Cheshire cat. "That isn't a problem, I called Mace." He held up his hand when it looked like Black was going to protest. "Relax. He knows Poe, who is Mr. Hart's assistant. Or at least, Bill knows Poe, I should say. Either way, Poe said he will put you down with a plus one. If you choose not to go, no big deal. But the option is there."

"When did you do all this, exactly?" Black asked, seeing as we all had just found out about it a few minutes ago.

"Ginger told Jones and me about it late last night. I got the idea to contact Mace about it while you and Quill were having your little powwow in here." He gestured to the leftover mess from Black's temper tantrum. "Poe was quick on the reply. If you want this, it can be done."

I peered over at Black, who was now staring out the window. "It's not a bad idea."

Was he serious? "You want to go out in public, to a ball, with me?"

Black whipped his head around, his golden braid swinging from one shoulder to the other. "Why wouldn't I? It won't raise any brows if I take a man to an LGBT ball."

While I was ninety-nine percent sure Black swung both ways, I wanted to be sure. "I didn't think you were gay."

"I'm not." He narrowed his eyes. "I'm bisexual. I can handle dancing with you."

"Dancing?" I squawked, and everyone chuckled.

"This will be fun. We can take the company card and go get you an amazing suit." Lana linked her arm with mine.

"But I have to work tomorrow night." I was taking in everyone's expressions, waiting for the *just kidding, you're not going* one. But no one said it.

"I'll handle that. Just find something. I will see you tomorrow night at six." He inched slightly closer to me. "Don't think we aren't going to talk more about things later."

Before I got a chance to say anything else, Lana was pulling me out of Black's office.

Chapter Thirteen

Black

Part of what made me so successful was knowing people's stories before they told me. Many lessons my father told me started with what he referred to as lawyer knowledge: never ask a question you don't know the answer to. Through my life, I'd altered that a bit. I liked to know their deepest secrets, darkest desires, and most sinful lies. With that knowledge, who they told me they were and who they actually were would never shock me.

Until recently, I'd had no need to dig into Quill's past. Fucking Ronald Sterling had planted that seed in my mind when he mentioned his brother, and that bloomed into a necessity when Quill had mentioned his family with so much disdain.

Lee had done a background check on Quill when he began running deliveries for me. Lee swore there was nothing fishy, and even though he didn't have a past we could blackmail him for, he wouldn't blink at working for me. I didn't ask more about it to Lee when he'd said that, and now I was very curious.

I asked Lee to stay behind as the others filed out; Lana and Quill off to shop, Jones and Ginger to work.

"What do you need?" Lee asked, eyes narrowed at the closed door.

"First, I will be addressing whatever issue you're having with Jones soon enough, so don't think the answer 'nothing is wrong' will fly. But right now, I need you to answer something for me."

Lee took a seat beside his still open laptop, waiting.

"When you did the background check on Quill, you

mentioned that he wasn't shady but he wouldn't argue over working for me, why?" Sitting behind my desk, I watched Lee's reaction to my question. He was generally stone-faced, but he flinched when I asked. It was tiny, but obvious.

"When you ask me to do background checks, I always know what you're looking for. Quill checked off all the boxes. He was fine. I didn't think airing his personal laundry was necessary." He held my gaze with a hint of defiance. He was defending Quill, and that wasn't typical of Lee unless it was for Jones.

"I respect you a great deal, Lee, but you have to admit, what happened to Quill recently could have his past rearing its ugly head. You know what that past is, so you can tell me if I'm wrong." I pointed to the door. "He mentioned a hatred for family. Ronnie said Quill's brother and family were worse. That's two factors."

He nodded, took a deep breath, and spoke. "Ronald wasn't wrong, and you're not either, about it possibly being a problem. And before I tell you what I know, understand I stopped digging after I read enough."

That was fair. "Fine, but you understand that I will be asking you to dig deeper."

"Yeah." Lee hit a few buttons on his laptop and began reading what I guessed was a written report. "Quill was actually born here in Haven Hart, lived here for about ten years. His father was killed by a gang on the steps of his bakery. Reports say it was due to the fact he used colors belonging to a gang here and refused to change them. It was about that time when Quill's life went to shit, because according to what I could find, his dad was the most stable person in his life."

Lee scrolled past what I figured was all the stuff he had already told me before continuing.

"He moved around a lot after that. His brother is five years older than him and worked at some shit places while his mother was a frequent flyer at many clinics and hospitals. I know this because I was able to hack into the Child Services sites and see that there were many visits for a Quill and a Dylan Almeida after their father's death."

Dylan. So that was Quill's brother's name. "Is his mother still alive?"

"No. She died of a heroin overdose when Quill was fifteen, leaving him in the care of his brother." The way Lee looked at me told me of dark times.

"So, for five years, Quill dealt with a drugged out, neglectful mother. What about his brother in all that time?"

"The brother stayed pretty clean, but Quill has some hospital records. Broken leg, two arm breaks, four times he went in for stitches." He shook his head. "Every time, Child Services was called, and every time, they ruled it a kids will be kids sort of thing."

One thing I knew was how the system failed the ones they were supposed to be protecting the most. It was a wonder Quill was still alive.

"Go on."

"There's a small gap. I assume it's where Quill must have run away, because the next thing I found was a slew of hospital stays here in Haven Hart. A lot over the last few years."

I wanted those records. I needed to see. "Did you get those?"

Lee chuckled. "It's funny, I can hack anything, any place Quill has ever lived, but I can't hack Haven Hart records. Bank or Hospital. I'm only able to ever get so far before I hit a wall."

Haven Hart was a fortress. It was one of the reasons I loved and loathed it so much. The Hart family protected this place like it was the best kept secret. We found out a few months ago, there were vaults below the city. Banks, hospitals, town hall. Mace and Bill were able to get inside one with the help of Poe, who was an aide to the Hart heir. The fact he was very good friends with Snow Manos worked in Bill's favor.

"Contact Bill. Tell him I need an email or something on Poe. I need to get into those vaults. I don't know how to get in contact with that man."

Lee nodded and began texting. I sat in silence. Waiting for some response, my mind wandered to the hell Quill had lived and the similarities to someone else I'd known once upon a time. The shiver of regret and guilt began to eat at me like it always did, and I was glad when Lee interrupted my dark thoughts.

"Bill sent over the email address and I'm forwarding it to you. He said it's the best he could do."

"Fair enough. I want you to dig into Dylan Almeida's life. Find out where he is. We need to see if he's living obliviously or if he's thinking of paying Quill a visit."

Lee began packing up his laptop and was heading out when I stopped him. "Before you go, what's going on with you and Jones?"

His shoulders sagged and a sad expression adorned his features. "I'd really rather not talk about it, boss."

I understood he didn't, we weren't emotional people. We had no time for it and it showed weakness.

"I wouldn't ask normally. I don't care if you two are fucking, but I do care that it's affecting my organization. So, you're going to have to give me something."

He placed his laptop bag by the door and sat on the couch. "Yeah, Jones and I have been sleeping together. It sort of just happened when we were on a job a few years ago. We never said we were together, never held each other up to a promise of monogamy. But…"

I knew where this was headed. The one place it never should have.

"You fell in love?" I asked.

"Yeah," he huffed. "Freaked Jones the fuck out when I said it. But I'd held it in for a long time. The second I said it, he closed up. Started flirting with others. I'm sure he's slept with others, too. I don't have proof. But we weren't exclusive. I couldn't get mad at him."

"But you did anyway?" I smirked, earning a chuckle.

"Yeah. He started avoiding me, and then with Ginger..." His head dropped forward in defeat. "I hate loving him, Black. It hurts too much."

This was why whenever I felt jealous of Riordan or Mace, I smacked myself with a dose of reality. Love was an undefeated beast. It would take down the biggest of people and bathe in their ashes.

"Don't you just wish you could un-love him?" I tried to be the person that helped others, especially my men, but in moments like this, I was on love's radar. It wasn't going to let me blindfold Lee, to turn him away.

"No, Black, I just wish he'd love me back."

After Lee left, I found myself almost useless. His words drummed through my head over and over. He didn't want to forget Jones, he wanted Jones to love him in return. Didn't he realize the pain love gave you was worse than the loneliness?

It was late when I finally left the office for my penthouse apartment. My place was too large for me and I was too stubborn to fill it. Normally, I'd sip some whiskey and go over the loads of work I didn't finish at the office, but tonight, I found I didn't care about any of it. Between Lee's heartache and Quill's heartbreak, my mind was chaotic.

I sat there all night, staring out the large windows that overlooked all of Haven Hart. Miles and miles of city. Past the skyscrapers, lived the quiet homes where love blossomed, children laughed, and I was far away from.

Chapter Fourteen

Quill

"Let me get this straight," Melissa said as she helped me tie all the garbage to go out. I was working a morning to afternoon shift at Quirks and Perks and normally would go over to Joker's Sin afterwards, but Black told me to just go home after here and get ready.

"What's confusing, Mel, is he asked me to go to a grand ball where a ton of rich, amazing people will be and he and I will dance into the night. And if I'm lucky, under a full moon, he will kiss me tenderly and tell me he will never let me go. AND," I shouted excitedly, lost in my fairytale, "a large, white steed will whisk us away to Hawaii."

Mel rolled her eyes and chuckled. "There's so much wrong with that, but I won't correct you."

"Appreesh," I said as I dragged a bag to the back door by the alley.

"You're forgetting, Bartholomew Sterling will be there, and he's inviting you because he wants to basically piss on your leg in front of the guy so his son will leave you alone. Not dreamy, Quill." She held the door open.

"I thought you said you wouldn't correct me?" I narrowed my eyes and slinked out the door, pulling two bags behind me. The bell chiming over the entry door had Mel going back to the front, leaving me to finish garbage duty alone. Fortunately, my wrist only twinged with pain, nothing lasting.

I'd just hauled the last bag into the dumpster when I heard it. Like a hum, or a whistle, or... *what the hell is that?* Following the sound, it led me to a heap of soggy boxes. The chill of winter kissed my skin as I got closer to the mouth of the alley.

"Hello?" I said, arms crossed, trying to protect myself from the icy mist that flowed my way. The sound stopped for a second, then it began again. This time it sounded like a wounded cry. What the hell?

Just using my pointer and my thumb, I began pulling the soggy cardboard apart. I lifted a disgusting pizza box when I saw it.

It couldn't have been bigger than my hand, perhaps a tad larger. It was gray and white, and its eyes were the prettiest shade of amber I'd ever seen.

"Oh my, what are you doing down there, little guy?" So slowly as to not scare the kitten, I reached down to pick him up. Sure, I wondered if he had rabies and if this was how my life ended, but I couldn't ignore his cries. "There you go, you're okay." He shook from fear or the cold, I didn't know. His left ear had a nick in it and there was dried blood on his paws. "You're okay. I'm Quill, nice to meet you. I'd ask your name, but I doubt you'd answer me." I walked back down the alley toward the café. Mel would likely yell at me for picking up a diseased stray and for going out without a coat, but I felt like a hero in this moment.

"What is that?" She pointed to the furball huddled close to my chest as I sat in the breakroom.

"A kitten. He was under a bunch of soggy boxes. Are you still friends with that vet guy, what's his name?"

"Yeah, why?" She knew where I was going with this, and she knew I knew, but apparently, we were playing this game... *Okay*.

"I want to keep him. He's sad and alone."

"Quill, you work three jobs. He's clearly seen hard times, he's going to need a lot of care. You aren't going to be able to help him." She sat beside me and carefully rubbed Kitty's good ear.

"Mel, I won't toss him aside. I know how that feels." Patting the crusty fur, I whispered, "He needs his prince too."

She was quiet for a minute, then she sighed and took out her cellphone. The warmth of victory felt good.

An hour later, she was pushing me out the door and ushering me into an Uber. "Do as the doc says and have fun tonight. I will be at your place after I close to watch the kitten." Her expression softened when she looked at the kitty. "We'll figure it out, Quill. Love you."

The whole way to the clinic, Kitty shook and meowed. I had money saved, mostly for if my brother ever showed up demanding it, but I'd risk even his wrath to save Kitty.

I had never been to the vet clinic. Sure, I'd been to enough hospitals and seen enough doctors of my own, but never one for animals. This was totally new for me.

Doctor Mason made me wish I was a cat. He was ridiculously hot. Taller than me, which was typical, he had thick salt and pepper hair, muscles that screamed "lick me," and those eyes, damn, no way they were that perfect shade of fuck-me blue.

"Quill, is it?" he asked in his body melting voice.

"Y... yes, Quill. This is Kitty." I held up the gray ball of despair for him to see.

"Oh dear!" The sheer look of horror and sadness on his face mimicked how I felt when I first saw him too. "Right this way."

Kitty was so good for Dr. Fuck Me, I mean Mason. The examination was thorough and I was glad the results were better than I feared.

"There's no question of malnourishment. Thankfully, the blood isn't Kitty's. Possibly, she ran from something…"

"Hold up." He'd said she. "You said she."

When he smiled, there were lines that showed me a lifetime of laughter and it was contagious.

"I did. He is, in fact, a she. I'd say Kitty is about eleven weeks. There's no bites or scratches, so I'm confident ruling out rabies. I'd like to keep her for at least several days. Wash her up, get her weight stabilized, and rehydrated. She needs a series of shots and I'd feel better if she was monitored." He petted Kitty and it was clear as she nuzzled up to the doctor, she was a whore, and totally mine.

"Okay, um… When would you say I could get her and what would I need to care for … a cat, Kitty? Is that a good name?"

Dr. Mason chuckled and reached into his jacket. "I'll write you a list so you can get her everything she needs. You'll have some time, and when I feel she's able to go home, I, or someone on my staff, will contact you."

"Thank you." I gave Kitty a kiss on her gross head and feeling lighter than I had in a while, headed out to the bus. It was three o'clock and Black was getting me in exactly three hours. I had to hustle if I was going to be on time.

I shot a quick text off to Mel letting her know that Kitty was staying at the clinic for a while and she didn't have to come by. I was glad because I had no idea how to make the security in my apartment not kill her when I wasn't there.

Back at my place, I grabbed the ridiculously expensive suit Lana and I had purchased, along with the cool new shoes, and laid them out, then hopped into the shower. I knew Mel was right that tonight was about warning the Sterlings away from me, but I was good at pretending and using my imagination. Tonight, regardless of what Black said, I was thinking of it as a date.

I glanced at myself in the floor length mirror and thought I looked really good. I only hoped Black thought so too.

Chapter Fifteen

Black

"We're here, sir," my driver said as we pulled up to Quill's building. I texted him that I was out front and proceeded to return a few texts from Jones and Lee while I waited.

We knew most of the Sterling family would be in attendance for the Rainbow Hart Charity Ball, which worked out well. There would be no misunderstandings about Quill being under my umbrella of protection. If they wanted to think he was my boyfriend, all the better. This way he would be safe. At least, I hoped.

I had just finished my text when I heard the car door open. A cheery hello from Quill had me glancing up and doing a double take. He had taken out most of his piercings, likely to fit in as best he could. His hair was still black and his eyes were a deep blue. Any chance of him blending in went right out the window with his suit.

It was the color of his eyes, and by the looks of it, crushed velvet. Jacket and pants both melded to his body like a second skin. For a moment, I wanted to reach out and touch it, wondering how soft it was.

On anyone else, the suit would have seemed absurd, but for reasons I couldn't articulate, it worked for him. He was going to stand out, and in this instance, it wasn't a bad thing.

My silence must have come off as disgust as I noticed Quill's crestfallen face and how he nervously rubbed his thigh as he sat in front of me in the limo. I didn't want him nervous. I needed him confidant, like this was a life he was used to.

"That's quite the suit," I said with a small smile, which he returned.

"Yeah? I wasn't sure. I mean, I fell in love with it when I saw it and Lana was all, 'try it on,' so I did, and yeah." His eyes darted nervously over the interior of the limo.

"It works for you. I'd never pull something like that off." It was true. I was a large man and didn't need help being seen in public.

"I like the classic tux. It is very you." He reached across, lightly fingering the silver pocket square. "Matches your eyes," he said softly, almost like he was talking to himself.

"Thank you."

Whenever in Quill's presence, I was always on edge waiting for his flirting that was often annoying. Sometimes, it bordered on inappropriate. It was something I worried about tonight, and while he seemed to be in the mindset that this was important, I still felt I needed to make some rules clear.

"We are about twenty minutes from The Camille, so I'd like to talk to you about a few things."

He nodded, sat back, and I was relieved when he gave me his undivided attention.

"First and foremost, Jones, Lee, and Ginger will be in attendance. You may or may not see them, but if you do, don't bring attention to them. They are keeping an eye out."

"Got it."

"Second, you don't go off with anyone while we're there without talking to me first."

Quill's brow crinkled. "I doubt I will know anyone there aside from you, your guys, and some of the Sterlings, and there's zero chance of me being alone with any of those fake assholes."

"Right, but if someone makes an offer or…"

"Wait just a minute." He held up his hand as anger morphed his sweet face. "Are you calling me a slut? You really think I'd go off for a quickie with some rich nub?"

Nub? "Quill, I'm just giving the black and white rules here, calm down."

He chuckled. "Right, sure, fine. Go on, Master."

"That sarcasm brings me to another important rule."

Quill leaned forward, irritation pouring off him like water. "I'm dying to know, sir, please tell me, sir."

"Don't make a spectacle of yourself by flirting cheesily or humping my leg." I was going to phrase it nicer, but his attitude was pissing me off.

"Cheesily isn't a word, and I'm not feeling very humpy toward you at the moment. Stabby, yes."

This was going to be a long night.

THE CAMILLE WAS by far the most expensive and opulent hotel in all of Haven Hart. It was to pay homage to a woman no one knows much about, but the extraordinary sight of the lobby alone tells anyone who enters that she was extremely important to the Hart family. When I was younger, I told my father I felt like I needed to pay my respects. He laughed and told me sometimes the extravagant hides the truths and to not think more on it. So, I didn't. For years, I simply walked the marble floor whenever I entered and stopped gawking at the gold and ivory.

I had every intention of doing that this time, but as we entered, I was brought to a sudden halt when Quill stopped walking. His head dropped back, taking in the heavenly ceiling that was reminiscent of Michelangelo's ceiling in the Sistine Chapel.

"Wow," his voice echoed in the lobby. A few desensitized

people walked past him, scrutiny adorning their faces. Of course, to Quill, this was outstanding. *He'd likely never been inside here.*

"It's amazing, isn't it?" Lightly, I took his arm and was glad when he slowly began following me toward the grand ballroom.

"I've never seen anything like it. We have a gorgeous mural in the book store above the café, but it's nothing like that. It's like looking into heaven almost." He spoke with so much reverence, I wished I could let him stay and appreciate it. But the laughter and sound of the orchestra playing not far from where we stood made that wish impossible right then.

"Perhaps when we leave, you can take a longer look." I tried for a soft smile as his blue eyes glistened and his face dropped. The reality of tonight, no doubt weighed on him.

"Right, yeah. Let's get this show on the road." He entwined his arm with mine, pasted on a perfect smile, and the determination in his poise made my earlier worries disappear. Of course, he would be great at masking his emotions. According to his file Lee gave me, he'd been doing it forever.

The grand ballroom was just that, grand. Being it was December, it was no surprise to see them work a Christmas theme into the LGBT one. Trees and wreaths covered the walls and the circumference of the ballroom. Each a symbol. Gay, bisexual, transgender, pansexual, intersex, Asexual, you name it, it was represented here tonight. The more I scanned the room, I saw all the religions were in attendance as well. It was diverse in every way. It made me more curious about the Hart heir to go all out for LGBTQA youth in this city.

"I feel like a broken record, but wow." Quill chuckled and gripped my arm tighter. "This is crazy."

I had to agree with him on that. I had been to many balls and galas in my time, but this one seemed to have almost a whirl of magic to it. The orchestra all dressed in rainbow tuxedos played soft music, likely to keep the mood calm for now. The tables all were a different color; red, orange, purple, and white. The room itself made it clear why we were all here. To help our LGBTQA youth.

"Shall we find our table?" I asked Quill, and he nodded absently as he continued to take in the room.

I was impressed with our table. It was along the dancefloor away from the kitchen entrance, and there was plenty of room for my large body.

"I wonder who we're sitting with." Quill pointed to the empty seats, and I hoped they weren't chatty and annoying.

"As long as Bartholomew Sterling sees us and I get a chance to speak with him, I don't much care who we're saddled with."

Quill shrugged and began to fidget with his suit. He tried to remain strong, but every so often, his nervousness showed.

"Why don't we walk to the bar, get a drink, and maybe by the time we return, we will see who our mysterious tablemates are?" I offered my hand, which he took like a lifeline.

"Yeah, a drink is a perfect idea."

My eyes scanned the entire ballroom, but I didn't spot any of the Sterlings. They likely would arrive fashionably late, or as I called it, irritatingly late.

At the bar, Quill ordered some fruity pop drink. He winked at the bartender and while I knew it was just his personality and not that he wanted to get in the guy's pants, I couldn't help the unease it brought me.

"Thor will have a Jack and coke, please."

"Thor?" My eyes widened, but the bartender just chuckled and left to retrieve my drink.

"Um, yeah. You remind me of Thor and a little like what I imagine Satan might look like." He smiled brightly as he took the tiny red straw into his mouth and sucked.

"Satan and Thor?" He nodded. "So, you think Satan is hot?" When he choked on his drink, the satisfaction of shocking him made me smile. I thanked the bartender as he placed my drink in front of me.

"I had no idea you could do that," he said in wonder.

"What, make a joke?" I gratefully took the drink the bartender handed me.

"No, not that. I had no idea you could smile."

Something about his tone had me stopping mid drink. Surely, I'd smiled in front of him before.

"You wear it well, Satan, you should do it more often." With that, I watched as Quill walked back to our table.

CHAPTER SIXTEEN

Quill

My mind was so cluttered with curiosity over Black's absolute flirting after he told me not to, I didn't even see two people take their seats at our table.

"Quill?" The sound of surprise and happiness caught my attention and I turned toward the most jovial person in the world.

"Teddy? What are you doing here?" I hadn't seen him a lot lately. After his almost dying of anaphylactic shock two years ago and him now being one of Black's former assassin's husband, he was quite busy and rarely came into the café anymore.

"It's such a long story," he chuckled. "I volunteer at the hospital, and my brother in-law is a doctor there. Anyway, he had an invitation to come to this with his wife but their daughter is sick, so he asked me to come and, well," he swept his hand over the room, "what an amazing reason to eat, drink, and be merry."

Teddy Harris, now Darcy I supposed, truly was one of those people you couldn't help but be happy around. He volunteered all over Haven Hart from abandoned babies to LGBTQA people. When he wasn't volunteering, he was running his own cuddling company. Yes, he hugged and cuddled people for a living. Take all that, and add to it the fact that he'd happened to snag a vicious assassin and make him turn his life around, and I was fairly certain he was going to become a saint.

"Now, your turn," Teddy urged me, but we were interrupted by Black and Riordan.

"I see you found my better half," Riordan said as he slipped a drink in front of Teddy and sat beside him with one of his own.

"It's great to see you, Quill. Black, here, was just telling me how he managed to wrangle you in to coming tonight with him."

Wrangled me? I thought for sure Black would tell Riordan what was happening and that this wasn't a date, just a way to keep the Sterlings off my back. As I tried to figure out how to answer him, Black came to my rescue.

"It wasn't easy. My date cancelled on me at the last minute. Fortunately, Quill was working right as the call came in and he took mercy on me." He shot me a wink and after the brief explosion of warmth in my lower belly subsided, I realized of course he wouldn't tell Riordan the truth. He didn't work for him anymore.

"Oh yeah, it's a real hardship getting all dolled up, being on the arm of a gorgeous man, and pretending to be anyone but me for a night." I tried playing the part, but it was Teddy who saw right through me.

"Why would you want to be anyone else but you?" he asked, curls bobbing as he cocked his head in question.

"Not tonight, babe," Riordan said. "No analyzing and trying to save souls tonight. Unless they're one of the kids we are here for."

I was glad when the conversation steered away from me. As Black and Riordan talked about some sort of new security system that some up and coming company was trying to sell, my eyes wandered the room. Aside from Teddy and Riordan, no one else was familiar. I wished the Sterlings would just arrive and Black could get on with the show, so maybe I could relax a little.

"Everything okay?" Teddy asked, and of course, he was watching me.

"It is. Thanks. How's married life?" I knew asking him anything about his own wonderful life would get him away from interrogating me.

"Great! Riordan is loving his security work. That he's home at a reasonable time is beneficial. We just bought a new place. And since he spent the last two years taking me all over the world showing me the places I wanted to see most, we have been thinking of adoption." He spoke fast and was smiling so brightly, I thought one of the passing waiters would ask him to turn it down.

"Wow, babies. That's... Well, I won't lie, Teddy, that's a nightmare for me, but yay for you."

He laughed so loudly, it caught the attention of those around us... and that was when I saw him.

Bartholomew Sterling was an imposing man. He wasn't broad and muscular like Black, but there was an air of superiority and power about him. He was tall, all sleek and shiny. His family was referred to as new money. After the death of Bartholomew's father, he inherited a fortune. He moved himself and his family over to Haven Hart a few years ago and brilliantly began giving to charities and showing their faces at worthy events. He had made all the right investments, supposedly, and opened his own advertising agency that took off like a house on fire. At least, that was what I'd heard, but who knows? He never seemed to be working, he was always out schmoozing.

It was no secret the Sterlings were looking at taking over the city, but there was always a power that thrummed through Haven Hart like a pulse. No one knew who the Hart heir was, but that almost made it mean more. Like he didn't have to be present to reap the rewards for his kindness, he just did. It was something the Sterling family would never understand, and because of that, they would always be second best.

I dated Ronnie for a year, on and off. It wasn't really a great relationship. It was at first, but I didn't fit the mold of what he wanted. Any time I met Bartholomew or Ronnie's mother, it was never pleasant. Often times, Ronnie was called away to speak with his father and I'd hear the words of disdain.

I stopped my relationship with Ronnie more times than I

could count, but it wasn't over for Ronnie unless he said it was. And so, this brought us to tonight. Black's master plan to show the Sterlings I was his and they needed to get their son under control... or else.

"You know the Sterlings?" Teddy asked, and that brought Black's head up and over. He stared at the man as he slunk across the dance floor to his table.

"Um... some."

"They are a family of philanthropists, I tell you. Angels. Just last month, they donated fifty thousand dollars to the neo-natal unit at Hart's Hope Hospital." Teddy was speaking like so many others did in this city. Oblivious to the evils that lurked behind the fake smiles and raven eyes.

"Money doesn't make you a savior." Black's voice was ominous and when he grabbed my hand, I knew it was game time. "If you'll excuse us, we're going to go over and say hello to the angels of Haven Hart."

"Oh, what a good idea!" Teddy began to stand, but Riordan stopped him.

"Not right now, Teddy. I don't think this is our moment."

It was obvious Riordan understood that whatever we were going to do, it wasn't charming or sweet. Something in Riordan's gaze must have clued Teddy in, because he sat back down and nodded.

"We'll be right back, I'm sure." I offered a smile I hoped appeased Teddy and followed Black's lead as we made our way into the belly of the beast.

Chapter Seventeen

Black

Bartholomew Sterling looked like a snake. I knew enough about him through Lee's research to know why I didn't rub shoulders with him. He was everything I hated in the world. He was why my past dictated my future. Men like Bartholomew and Ronald traipsed into places dazzling the naive with their glitter and charm, all the while setting fire to those very people's livelihoods. Men like them were illusionists, not philanthropists like Teddy had said.

I understood there were many rich and powerful people in Haven Hart. Most should be happy I wasn't aware of their names and faces. Only those I needed to watch did I make it my business to know. And now, because of Bartholomew's piece of shit son, the Sterlings were very much on my radar.

I knew Quill was nervous. I knew I had snapped at him in the limo, likely making the situation worse. I tried to add levity to the situation by mildly flirting, but that might end up being a mistake later. Now, as we got closer to the snake himself, I felt Quill's sweaty palm in mine and the hesitation in his steps.

There was a crowd of people surrounding the Sterlings, so I took a moment and turned toward Quill. His blue eyes widened with trepidation. The tremble in his body vibrated through me, and without pause, I pulled him into my embrace. In that moment, as we were ironically in the middle of the dance floor, the orchestra began a gorgeous rendition of Silent Night and I used this time to calm him.

"Dance with me," I leaned down and whispered in his ear. He stood stock still for a moment, then with a nod, he relaxed.

Quill was so much smaller than me, I was able to wrap myself around him. And in that moment, as I felt the fear flutter through his body, I wanted to do just that. Memories of a time I was desperate to save someone so much like Quill filled my mind. The desperation, need, and terror of realizing I couldn't.

"I can't breathe." Quills words were muffled in my chest.

"Sorry." Pushing him back, I took one of his hands in mine and placed my other on his hip. He let me lead without protest, and as the melody floated through the ballroom, I glided over the oak dance floor with this annoying and, yes I admitted, beautiful man.

I was glad to see him smile and giggle as I spun him. And by the time the song came to an end, he was fully relaxed.

"I promise you're safe, Quill. I will make everything right so you don't ever need to be afraid again." My words felt more like a plea.

Quill's eyes softened, his lips curled, and the slender hand he placed on my rough cheek thawed something in me.

"You're going to be my Prince, Black? Powerful like Thor and as dark as the Devil?" It was a silly thing to ask. Something out of fairytales, and those weren't real. "I know you're used to getting your way and fighting the battles for the broken. But even Thor doesn't win them all. And sometimes, Satan has to concede."

I had no idea what he was saying, but I did know he was doubting I could protect him.

"Come on, let's show the Sterlings they aren't as big as they think they are."

Resignation painted Quill's face. He gripped my hand and as we got closer to Bartholomew Sterling, the circle of people surrounding him dispersed. The snake himself stared at Quill, his eyes focused coldly, only to narrow when he saw me attached to his arm.

"Bartholomew Sterling?" I asked respectfully, hand raised to shake. He returned it, eyes shifting between me and Quill.

"I am, and you are?"

"Allow me to introduce myself. I'm Terrance Blackrose."

The reaction was more than I could have hoped for. His smile brightened and he actually pressed the lapel of his jacket to iron out the nonexistent wrinkles.

"Oh, Mr. Blackrose, it's wonderful to finally make your acquaintance. This is my wife, Wanda." A woman with platinum blonde hair in a classic French twist and more makeup on than needed raised a limp hand to me.

"Pleasure," she said disinterestedly. Her bright red dress was one a twenty-year-old would wear and it would look elegant. On her, it was all wrong. She was an older woman who was internally screaming to be young. It was almost sad. But, with all his money, I was sure no one would dare tell her that.

"This is my date, Quill Almeida." Quill rolled his eyes and I thought he was going to say something awful, but instead, he lifted his hand, looked Bartholomew in the eyes, and with a steady voice, exclaimed they had met.

"Is that right?" I spoke in a mocked tone and it was in that moment, Bartholomew seemed to catch on, so I went in for the strike. Speaking in hushed tones so only the four of us could hear, I said, "Let this be the only time we speak, Mr. Sterling. If your son comes anywhere near Quill, I will kill him with my bare hands. If he doesn't accept the charges against him for assaulting Mr. Almeida, I will kill him. And if he threatens to do anything that could later cause harm to Quill..." I raised a brow. "I think you get it."

"How dare you speak to us—" Wanda began, but Bartholomew placed a hand on her arm, silencing her.

"You are aware Quill Almeida is a whore, right? He will take from you everything he needs and leave you a heap on the floor.

You'll wake wondering what happened and by then, it will be too late. He's trash and you're a fool if you think he won't do the same to you." His eyes shifted to Quill. "You broke my son's heart. He reacted because of that and you'll twist that knife further?"

"Are you fucking high?" Quill's voice rose more than I would've liked, but when he spoke again, it was softer, realization that others would overhear compelling him. "Your son is an abuser. Hit me even when we were together, and don't you two act like you didn't know. Hell, I heard you and Ronnie talking all the time about me, so you can take your priggish, wanna-be posh ass and suck it."

"Oh, yes, you certainly told me." Bartholomew's attitude wasn't filling me with any amount of joy. "My son will fight those charges. His character compared to that of your—"

"Quill Almeida is my partner, boyfriend, so be very careful what you say next, Mr. Sterling."

"Hmmf, very well. Once we dig into your boyfriend's past, I'm sure any judge will see the quality of stock each comes from. Not to mention…" He directed his next words to Quill. "I'd make sure we called character witnesses, family perhaps?"

I wasn't sure Quill's pallor could get any whiter. There weren't many times my plans went topsy turvy, and while this wasn't a failed mission, Bartholomew Sterling was going to make it difficult.

"Very well, Mr. Sterling, but remember something very important." Inching even closer, reveling in the nervous swallow I watched glide down his neck, I whispered, "The circles I hang out in aren't the law. I gave you your one and only chance. You should've taken it."

I took Quill's arm and gently guided him away from the bastard.

Chapter Eighteen

Quill

Oh my god. Oh my god. Oh my god. All the way back to our table, those three words played over and over again in my head. Black was making everything worse. Why had I agreed to any of this?

"It's a mere speedbump. This is clearly never going to see a courtroom, which is fine by me," Black said softly, but I heard him.

"What do you mean?"

I saw Teddy and Riordan dancing and offered a shaky wave as they both smiled at us as we passed to go to our table.

"Nothing you need to worry about."

"Maybe if I file a restraining order? I should. The officer that night told me to do it and I didn't listen."

Black halted and turned to face me. "Is that how you want to handle this? You want to do the restraining order, go in front of a judge who will look at you and then smile at Ronnie and his family, shrug, and let him go free? You want to look over your shoulder, forever begging the authorities to help you, only for them to finally give a shit when it's too late?"

Black was far from unhinged, but he gripped my shoulders roughly, not painfully. His eyes shimmered with anger laced in worry. I knew in my bones he wasn't mad at me and was seconds from walking over to Bartholomew, punching him in the face and ending his life.

"I already look over my shoulder, Black. That doesn't change with the outcome of this." Black narrowed his eyes. "Don't give me that face. My life hasn't been the best, but I know how to survive."

"By getting the shit kicked out of you constantly?"

I didn't know how to answer that. I was alive and knew I'd stay that way as long as I didn't make too many waves and did as I was told.

"Maybe by getting the restraining order, it will scare the Sterlings enough. They will see their shiny future begin to tarnish and not want that. I bet Bartholomew will demand his son stay away from me then."

He shook his head and took the last few steps back to our table.

"What?" I asked as I sat beside him. "You told Bartholomew to make Ronnie accept the charges and be responsible. That's no different than what I'm saying."

"Except he said no."

A waiter came by and took our drink and dinner order. Teddy and Riordan returned in time to place theirs as well. I wanted to talk to Black more about this, but our table was filled and the festivities were underway.

A tapping of a mic drew our attention. A brunette woman stood behind a podium, waiting for the room to quiet down.

"Thank you all so much for attending this year's Rainbow Hart Charity Ball. The Hart family thanks you greatly for your generosity this evening and to speak on the family's behalf, I want to welcome Edgar Ravens." The room burst in applause and a man I'd seen before took the stage. His long, black hair was tied back in a ponytail, his alabaster skin practically lit up under the stage lights, and thick, dark glasses adorned his face. He wore a simple tuxedo and thanked the woman before making his way to the podium.

"That's Poe, isn't it?" Teddy asked. "I didn't know his real name was Edgar Ravens, did you?" he asked Riordan, who shook his head. "Interesting. I'll have to ask him tomorrow at the park."

I didn't know what Teddy was talking about, my eyes were drawn to the now smiling man facing the room.

"I go by many names as most of you can see, but that's the thing with nicknames, you don't get to pick them and they alter people's perceptions." The room chuckled.

"As the liaison for the Hart family, I am honored to have you all here to help raise money for such a well-needed cause. LGBT youth worldwide need open arms, and if I'm honest, overflowing pocketbooks." He smiled as the room chuckled once more.

"The statistics on our youth change daily. Much of our society think that because of the year we live in and the growing diversity that there isn't a problem, or at least, it's not as serious. It's thoughts like that that stall progress."

He wasn't wrong. Every day, the stats changed, and often in the coffee shop, I'd hear people talk about how much better the world was and how there wasn't as much of a problem. It was what made people stop helping.

"The Hart family wants everyone in this great city to feel loved and cared for. I am hopeful that one day, there won't be a hungry belly or a homeless person in existence. I'm aware I'm an optimist, but someone has to be."

Light cheers filled the room and as I scanned the tables, everyone was enamored by the man on stage.

"Today Haven Hart, tomorrow the world. Let's lead by example. Let's make Haven Hart the arms our LGBT youth need wrapped around them. With that, others will follow and in time, maybe, just maybe, we can rid ourselves of the hate."

It was such a beautiful thought. One that was deserving of the standing ovation. Right before he got off the podium, he spoke again. "I also want to thank Xander Vayne for volunteering his outstanding culinary skills to you all tonight. Your food has been prepared by his restaurant, Vayne, which just opened on Fifth Avenue. After tonight, I'm sure you'll all be checking it out."

A man in a chef's outfit shook Edgar's hand. I couldn't see much since he only graced us with a profile, but his hair was so dark it was almost blue, and his body was, well, I didn't know because it was covered in baggy clothes. With a quick wave, he ran off back to his kitchen and light music began to play again.

Our food came out shortly thereafter, and as promised, it was amazing. I was desperate to get Black alone and ask him some questions, but as the night went on, speeches were made, and so much talking was had, we didn't get out of there until midnight. I knew he'd drop me off at home and I'd never get to ask my questions.

"I have assigned a car for you," Black said as his limo left the hotel.

"What?"

"Until things die down, I don't want you walking around this city as easy prey. You're safe inside your apartment and Clive is not just a driver, he works security for me. He will be here when you need to go somewhere." He handed me a card. "Put his number into your phone." He whipped his head toward me, his gaze piercing through me. "Don't ignore this."

I couldn't say no if I tried. "Um, okay, sure."

"Thank you."

I slipped the card into my pocket and stared out the window. The snow was falling lightly and my mind drifted to my new kitty. Oh!

"Black?"

"Hmm?" he asked as he read something off his phone.

"Can you ask Lee how to stop my security system from killing my cat when she gets home?"

He plopped the cell on his lap and raised a brow. "A cat?"

"Yeah. I don't want Kitty to get shot with a dart every time she goes to eat."

He chuckled and I really loved it. "Animals aren't programmed in, your cat will be safe."

"Oh phew. I wouldn't want Kitty to die."

"Kitty? That's her name?"

I shrugged. "Yeah, why, is it stupid?"

He made a face that showed he didn't want to hurt my feelings. There was a little blubbering, a hand gesture or two.

"It's stupid. Okay. I will think on it."

When Black dropped me off, he told me to be safe and he'd call me tomorrow for a meeting to go over all that needed to be done in regards to Ronnie. I knew that would be my moment to ask Black what had him reacting the way he had tonight.

CHAPTER NINETEEN

Black

"According to my friend in the courthouse, the Sterlings' lawyer has been like a Pitbull over this situation with Quill. Bartholomew wasn't lying when he said he'd fight this," Lana said as she placed a fresh cup of coffee on my desk. It was nine in the morning and we were going over our day. Lana pretty much attacked me when I got off the elevator, asking how the ball was and who was there and what happened.

"I've dealt with men bigger than him, Lana. They use all their fireworks before it's even dark outside. We will be patient. Call my lawyer and get the restraining order and all that set up."

She quirked a brow at my mention of forms and proper channels. "You hate authority, and for good reason. You never use it and would rather cut your arm off than rely on the judicial system, so why the change of heart?"

Knowing Lana as long as I had was a benefit in a lot of ways. I didn't have to explain to her why I had no use for the law, she'd seen me at my worst. She was loyal to a fault. The down side was all those things as well.

"I am not having a change of heart, but I will make the Sterlings think I am doing it the lawful way…" I was about to continue when the sound of shouting came from the other side of my door. It was near impossible for danger to reach my floor, so it had to be in house.

I told Lana to stay put while I checked it out. When I opened the door, Jones and Lee were facing off. Ginger sat in an office chair with a look of frustration on his face.

"Maybe if you weren't fucking around with the gingerbread man here, you wouldn't have failed at your job," Lee snapped at Jones. Ginger shook his head, and I had enough.

"That's enough. We're settling this right fucking now." I could tell the authority in my voice was all that was needed to get them to snap out of it. "Lana, we will continue this later. Please let Quill know what we discussed about the papers and I will get in touch this week for that meeting instead."

"You got it." She left, silently rolling her eyes behind the Three Stooges' heads.

Jones, Lee, and Ginger had the decency to keep their eyes downcast as I took my seat behind my desk.

"Let me make one thing very clear to the three of you. What I just witnessed should have never been seen." Ginger was about to speak, but my raised hand stopped him. "Now, since you want to act like five-year olds, I will treat you as such. When I point to you, tell me what happened. The first to interrupt anyone will wish they hadn't."

I had worked with Jones and Lee for so many years, I was curious what Ginger had to say about this, so I pointed to him.

His eyes widened in surprise. He likely thought I'd choose the others because I had known them longer.

"Well," he began. "According to the schedule, Jones was supposed to be watching the cameras for Quill. He needed to use the bathroom, and when he peeked out and saw me, he asked me to come in. We talked for a second and when we turned to the cameras, the screens were black."

Suddenly, I didn't give a shit about much of anything. Quill was in danger. "And your tiff was more important than Quill's safety?"

I made to hit the button to get Lana to order a team over there when Ginger spoke again. "We sent out Team X to find out what happened."

I was in no way appeased, not even a little bit. "Continue," I rumbled, my anger barely contained.

"So, we reported it and Lee came in, saw the two of us, and shooed us out of the way. Got the cameras online, but when he did, the apartment was empty. We called Clive, but he said Quill never contacted him for pick up." Ginger sighed, eyeing both men. "Lee accused Jones of thinking with his dick instead of the job at hand. Jones called Lee a prima donna." He rolled his eyes. "I don't honestly know where I fit into this, sir."

"Quill is unaccounted for?" I turned toward Lee, who confirmed it. "Ginger, are you sleeping with either of these men?" He shook his head. "Then you can leave. Contact Team X and find out the situation."

He ran out of the room like his pants were on fire. I could feel the blood rushing to my face. The clench of my fists did nothing to sedate the tension rolling off me.

"I am so disgusted with the two of you. As of today, you are both on leave. I will contact you both on the future of your employment with me." Jones slammed his hand against the chair, but my glare halted his speech. "No. There's nothing either of you can say to make this okay. Jones, you stepped away from the computers when you should have called it in. You left your post." Equally angry, I faced Lee. "Your jealousy is compromising missions. You two figure it out, but do it away from me and away from my businesses. You both better hope Quill is okay or your suspension will be a termination and I don't mean your jobs."

I rotated my chair to face the window. I had no more words for them and didn't want to hear anything they had to say. It wasn't until I heard my door shut when I faced back around.

A few minutes later, there was a knock on my door and Ginger opened it, sticking his head in.

"Come in."

He stood at my desk and cut to the chase. "Team X arrived at the apartment. No sign of Quill, but no struggle and the security system wasn't activated, indicating no unwanted presence was on the property."

"And?"

"They are still looking for him."

I woke my computer up and signed in. Quill's schedule was available to me, and all I could see was he had to work at Joker's Sin this evening.

"Let the team leader know Quill is scheduled to work at Joker's Sin tonight at ten. If no one finds him before then and he's okay, that is where he will be."

He nodded and left.

By five, there was still no word. Melissa, Quill's friend, said she had spoken with him this morning and he likely went to the vet to check on his cat. It was confirmed he had gone there but had left after an hour, sans cat. Atlas said Quill didn't call out, so I expected he'd arrive at Joker's Sin as expected.

"Lana, I'm heading out. I'm going to meet Team X at the club. Yes, before you ask, I will let you know when we find him." She smiled and was distracted by the phone ringing. I left her to it and made my way to the garage to drive home to dress for Joker's Sin.

I tried desperately to ignore the niggle in the back of my mind that something was wrong. Flashes from the past played like a flipbook in my mind. I wanted to find Quill and I needed him to be okay.

I dressed similar to the last time I had gone there. Grabbed my leather jacket, then called my driver to meet me downstairs. It was only nine, but I wanted to see Quill walk into the place and know he was fine.

With Team X in place at eight, if he had arrived earlier, I would have known.

I WONDERED what theme Atlas was going for with all of the feathers, glitter, and stars hanging from the ceiling. I ordered a Jack and coke and stared the door down like I was going to fight it.

Five minutes to nine, I breathed what felt like my first breath in hours. I watched as Quill smiled at the bouncer by the door, his body sinuously dressed in a tight, white material that shimmered. His hair was gunmetal gray, the normally black bracelets he always wore replaced with shiny silver ones. I couldn't hear what they were talking about, but the laughter that fell from his mouth filled me with relief, a reassuring calm. He was safe.

I couldn't take my eyes off him as he slipped through the crowd. He was only a few feet in front of me when his color-of-the-day, stunning white eyes locked with mine.

"Black," he gasped. "Are you okay?"

"Am I okay?" Realizing my voice was rising, I collected myself. "I've been looking for you all day."

He didn't look ashamed or upset; he was clearly confused. "But I don't understand."

How could he not understand? "Where did I lose you in my statement?"

He scanned the room with his white eyes. It wasn't busy yet, so he gestured for me to follow him. We walked down a narrow corridor and turned to a room. Chairs and tables were all that filled it. He punched his number in and rounded on me.

"Don't come into my place of work and treat me like a kid. You told me to leave my apartment and tell no one where I was going, to keep to my schedule, so I did that, and now you're yelling at me?"

What the.... "I never told you to do that. Why would I tell you to leave the one place you were most safe?"

"Yes, you did. I got a call, listen." He took out his cell and played the voice mail. Sure enough, a voice sounding a lot like mine urged Quill to grab a few things, tell no one where he was going, and stay there until he had to go to work.

"I never made that call, Quill."

It had just dawned on Quill that he had done exactly what whoever on that message wanted when a loud boom came from outside. Not in the club, but from outside the building. Grabbing Quill, I raced down the corridor. Team X was right there.

"We need to get out of here," the leader, Malcom, said.

"What was that?" I asked as I followed behind him, Quill's hand in mine.

"Car bomb." Just as he said that, another explosion was heard. "Make that two."

"Ronnie?" Quill shouted through the screams of patrons.

"No way, not the Sterlings' style," Malcom said at the same time I also said no.

When we exited the building, a black van was waiting. "Go to your safe house," Malcom directed, and it was by far the best place to go.

With Team X taking point on this, I concentrated on being vigilant and keeping Quill safe.

Chapter Twenty

Quill

I had a million questions racing through my head as we drove to Black's home. I wanted to ask each one, but the anger radiating from Black was enough to keep my inquisition at bay until we were settled.

"I want a team at my place. It may be safe, but until I know what exactly is happening, I'm taking no chances," Black ordered to the driver, who nodded and continued driving.

I had no idea who Black was texting, but the speed in which his fingers danced over the screen was impressive.

"I bet you give autocorrect a run for its money." I hadn't meant to say anything out loud.

"What?" He never took his eyes away from his phone.

"Nothing, just, not that you're fat, but you're not small and your fingers type so fast, I assumed you made a million errors and autocorrect just, well, never mind." Shutting up, I opted for the scenery out the window. A gentle touch on my leg surprised me. Black's phone was on the side of his leg and he was giving me his full attention.

"I used to know this person who talked about ridiculous things out of nowhere when they were nervous. I spent so much of my life brushing it off until it was too late." He stopped talking. I wasn't sure if he was surprised he had shared that little morsel with me, but I sure as shit was. "Anyway, my point is, I know you're scared and maybe I'm just realizing it now, but you do it a lot. You mask your emotions with humor or pointless conversation."

There was no room for insult, I knew he was stating fact because that was who I was. It wasn't intentional, I had just lived this way for so long, I accepted that side of me. But I wore it like a shield and wasn't ready to lower it just yet.

"Two car bombs just went off where I work, a stranger pretending to be you ripped me from my safe place, and now I'm in a van headed to your home with nothing," I huffed. "I think it's safe to say I'm scared."

He just nodded, never looking away until the driver asked if he wanted him to park in the garage or go around back. The car began driving up a mountain, or maybe a big hill. As I peered out the window, I could see the Hart estate many miles away at the top of a very large mountain.

"You live up here?"

"Sometimes. I have a penthouse in the city. I was going to originally take you there, but Team X thinks it's too close to everything, so I'm taking you to my house. I don't come here often, only when I want to get away." He slipped his phone into his pocket and I was about to say more when we reached the top and the most gorgeous place I'd ever seen came into view.

It was a large, modern-day mansion. Windows surrounded the place, but I couldn't see through the glass. It was dark, so I couldn't tell if the outside was gray, black, or wood, but there was an eclectic elegance that was evident. The garage door opened and when we drove through the doors, I assumed we'd stop, but the driver kept driving down a slope and suddenly, I felt like we were going down to the Batcave or something.

Black chuckled and I turned toward him. "What?"

"You. You're surprised, aren't you?"

"It's just… Are you Batman?"

Black's laughter practically shook the car. Seeing him smile or laugh wasn't common and it lasted until the driver stopped the car.

"Come on," Black chuckled as he exited. The garage was insane. There were two lines of cars, motorcycles, and what looked like covered jet skis. I knew Black had a lot of money, but seeing it took my breath away.

Unworthy was a weird feeling. I stood beside his car as he and his driver walked away, and stared at my reflection in the chrome pillar. Grayish hair, white eyes, and matching alabaster, tight-fitting clothes. My bracelets glimmered in the lighting. Clean. But I felt dirty, like I didn't belong here. Dylan spent years telling me there was no place in the world for me. That my worth was to make his life easier. I believed it sometimes, but mostly realized he said it to be cruel. At this moment, I felt he was right.

"What's wrong?" I hadn't heard Black walk back to me so I jumped, and to my embarrassment, squeaked.

"Sorry. I'm coming." I wiped my sweaty hands on my pants and shuffled forward.

A small elevator opened and the two of us stepped in. The driver waved us off as he went a different direction and, in the confines of the elevator, I had nothing to say. The shaking I'd felt as we got into the van had subsided, but was replaced with inadequacy.

We rode in silence; Black's head rested against the mirrored wall and I spent the time appreciating the beauty of the man.

When the elevator opened, it was like being thrust into a fictional world and I was Dorothy in The Wizard of Oz when she stepped out of her black and white world and into a world of color.

"Fuck me," I whispered under my breath, apparently not softly enough.

"I will take that as a compliment." Black brushed past me and headed down two steps that led to a huge living room. The walls were all windows and the view was worth a billion dollars, which it wouldn't have surprised me if that was what he had paid for it.

"Can anyone see inside?"

He shook his head. "I love a good view, but I could literally press my body against the glass and no one on the outside would ever know."

That visual would be stuck in my head forever. Sweet god, this material wouldn't cover an erection… *think about soggy bread, that time you accidentally saw your dad naked…* There we go, that finally did it.

After calming myself, I couldn't help the gasp that broke free. "Is that?" I took a few steps and looked down. "A conversation couch? For real?" I loved these. They weren't common anymore since they were a big seventies thing, yet Black made this look modern.

"Yes. My grandmother had one when I was little and I remember she would fill the area with stuffed animals and we'd jump from one side to the other. Often, we missed and that was where the stuffed animals came into play." He smiled wistfully, and I got lost thinking what Black looked like as a little kid. No question, he was adorable.

"I'd totally take the table out and fill it with balls, then jump in them," I laughed, and Black's smile drooped.

"I had a friend who sometimes hung out at my grandmother's, she often said she wanted to do that too." He stared at the black, leather conversation couch, clearly lost in a memory.

I hopped down deep into the couches and patted the space beside me. "Is this the same person that I remind you of?"

I had no idea Black's coloring could turn so gray. "I don't really want to talk about it. I need to check in with the teams and…"

"No. You keep talking about it here and there and that tells me you do want to tell me, and your teams will contact you if there's something to report. Stop trying to get out of it and tell me who I remind you of."

I wanted him to want to tell me more, so I stayed silent as his eyes scanned the amazing view, then his phone. When he took the step down to the couch, I breathed in relief. I didn't know how or why Black seemed to shift, but he wasn't pushing me away anymore and I couldn't help wondering if it was because his past was colliding with the present and I was smack in the middle of it.

"We, I, may need a drink to get through this." He pointed to the bar behind me. It was gold and crystal and where it should've been gaudy, it was elegant.

"What's your poison?" I leaped up, shuffled to the bar, and grabbed a tumbler.

"Grab two glasses and the bottle of Jack."

Ahh… One of those stories. I collected everything, went back to sit beside him, and waited until he poured us both some liquid courage. It didn't take Black long to start talking.

"Her name was Sunshine and I fell in love with her the day she stole my pink crayon in Mrs. Cary's class. We were five and I knew in that second, I'd give her all the crayons she ever wanted if she always smiled at me like she did that day. And I did. I gave her everything, everything in my power. But my power wasn't enough."

It was like lead had dropped in the pit of my stomach. This story was going to change who Black and I were to each other. I was going to learn why Black was who he was and why he did what he did. I felt it deep in my bones like an anguished ache begging to be freed.

Chapter Twenty-One

Black

I didn't know why I thought telling Quill about Sunshine was the right thing, I just did. With everything going to shit around us, we were safe here, waiting, and when he looked at me with his color-of-the-day eyes, I saw something there. Understanding. I knew he'd get it and accept why I lived how I did. Lana knew, but only because she had met Sunshine, briefly, but she had met her and knew how when the end came, it made everything darker. She witnessed the beast that broke free after my world fell apart.

"Sunshine never really liked to play with the other kids but for some reason, she seemed to enjoy my company. We ate together, played together, did it all. We were content with it just being the two of us. We were like that until we entered middle school. I turned eleven same as she had, and we went into a different school. That was when things started to change."

I saw Quill scoot closer out of the corner of my eye, ready to likely hug me at some point.

"Sunshine's dad died that year, a heart attack. Her mom took it real hard and started drinking. She told me one day on the bus, she hadn't eaten dinner the night before because her mom had passed out before going to the store. So, I gave her my lunch and said to eat it, I'd grab hot lunch. Still, nothing really computed as there being a problem. I just thought her mom was having a tough go of things."

I closed my eyes and remembered sitting on the bus with her that day. The sun hit her golden hair and a stripe ran across her face, making her look like her namesake. Her smile rivaled the beam itself. It was the face I always saw when I needed to remember who she really was.

"For a few years, she seemed okay, quieter than most, but I asked once and she said she was a woman now. I was dumb enough to ask her what that meant and I got an unwanted lesson in a woman's menstrual cycle."

This made Quill laugh and it was contagious enough to make me join in.

"On her fourteenth birthday, she came to school in a cast. She said she was so excited for her birthday the night before, she ran down the stairs, slipped, and fell. I carried all her books and did all I could for her for the weeks she had it on."

"You were a great boyfriend." Quill smiled, but the sadness that surrounded his eyes told me he knew where this was going.

"A month later, she told me her mother was remarrying and I remember thinking how sad she was over it. I figured it was because she missed her dad, but as soon as her mother remarried, Sunshine began to wither away." I gulped my drink down, grateful when Quill poured more.

"She got a broken leg at one point, then a bruise by her eye. She was absent so much. This went on for a year and I begged my father constantly to do something. I knew something was wrong. He had Blackrose Securities, so I asked him to make use of it and help her."

"I was elated when he said he would contact his people on the force and get someone over there. I thought she'd be okay."

"How old were you at this point?" Quill asked so quietly.

"Fifteen." Again, I drank down my bourbon and again, Quill refilled it.

"The cops were called multiple times after that with no results. Never arrested her mom or stepfather. And all my dad would say is 'the law was a tricky thing.'"

I shook my head, the familiar feelings I had buried deep began to surface. Remembering was a vicious beast and the more I uncovered about Sunshine, the sharper the torment.

"One night, it was like two in the morning, my phone rang. It was her asking me to meet her at the train station. She asked for a bunch of stuff and I brought it with me. She sat huddled on the bench, her lip swollen, one eye was bloodshot, and she cradled her arm. She said she couldn't do it anymore and was going to go to her grandmother's in Maine."

"She was a survivor, Black, or at least, she wanted to be." Quill rubbed his hand over my arm, the connection giving me an odd sense of peace.

"I think she wanted to live in that moment. I told her I'd miss her and watched as she rode out of my life. One year later, just a month after my seventeenth birthday, she returned. I was so excited to see her, but at the same time not. She was but a shadow of the person I had known. Her golden hair was black, her eyes dull. She had gotten hooked on every drug she could and was only home because her grandmother couldn't handle it anymore."

"Oh no." Quill wrapped his arm around me as best he could and laid his head on my shoulder.

"I begged her to stay with me, promised to get her healthy and take care of her. I remember telling her I would always love her and wanted to die old and gray beside her." I tried to shrug away the familiar agony. "It was all true, I really wanted all that, but she wasn't in a good place."

We sipped our drinks, giving me a moment to calm down before I continued.

"The abuse became more severe. And I called the cops every time. Each time, they said there wasn't anything they could do since no charges were being pressed," I scoffed, fucking worthless pieces of shit. "Like they couldn't see he was beating the shit out of her or that her mom was ignoring it, they just didn't give a shit."

"This was here in Haven Hart?"

"Yeah, a different time, maybe, but it was right here where we live."

Another gulp of my drink and I wished it would numb me, but the more I unraveled, the more powerful the throb in my heart became.

"One night, the flashes of red and blue through my bedroom window woke me. Sunshine lived a few houses down from me and, of course, that was where the ambulance, fire trucks, and police cars were. In just my pants, I raced out the door and ran down the street. I knew the cops would try and stop me, so I climbed up the tree on the side of the house and slipped through her window. It was vacant and I heard voices downstairs. A woman walked down the hall and I followed to where she had come from. It was the spare bedroom. I will never forget what I saw that night. It's the reminder I need that the law doesn't protect, that you can't trust it to do the right thing, and that all their red tape gets in the way."

Quill pressed my shoulder, so I laid against the back cushions. He straddled my lap and with both hands cupping my cheeks, forcing eye contact, he asked, "What did you see? Let it all out, let someone else carry your burden."

I had heard that before. Girlfriends and boyfriends asking me to open up to them, to share and let them help, and none of them felt right... Or was it worthy? So how did Quill become the person, the one I knew would feel my pain? Was it because he reminded me of Sunshine? Was it because I hoped I could save him where I couldn't save her? I wasn't sure. What I was sure of was for the first time since I had met Quill, I wanted him to wrap himself around me. I wanted to lose myself in him and hope he released my demons.

"She was on the bed, blood all around her. I could see shallow breaths in the rise of her chest, but she was almost unrecognizable. Chains hung from the bed post; it was something out of a horror movie."

Quill's fingers tenderly stroked my jaw and slid through the strands of my beard, pushing little jolts of strength through my flesh.

"I whispered her name, saw her jump slightly, and in that brief movement, I stopped caring who saw or heard me." Quill and I both exhaled at the same moment. Quickly, I breathed in, hoping I could gather his air and it would fill me with the courage I needed to get to the end of this story.

"She was dying. The woman who left her there was a minute behind me, likely getting a gurney, something. But I knew she was dying. There was so much blood, all hers." A warm tear slid down my face, stopped by Quill's still finger, like he wasn't allowing it to drop.

"She whispered for me to take her away from here. So I did just that. I scooped her up in my arms. Her blood covered my chest and I felt my pants absorbing it. It felt like I only had minutes left with her, but I hoped for more."

"They just let you leave with her?" Quill's eyes were wide and his chin quivered like he wanted to cry but wouldn't.

"They tried to stop me, but it was my father who made it so I could pass. He shouted at the police, telling them they had had all the chances to save her. And if they couldn't do right by her in life, they didn't deserve the honor of her death."

Quill's lip quirked up. "Your dad sounded amazing."

"He was, mostly."

"Where'd you take her?" Quill asked as he resumed stroking my cheek.

"My house, my bed." Shit, it felt like the world was crashing around me just like that night. I carried her alone, unable to protect her, but I wasn't alone this time. It was like Quill was an impenetrable blanket, not letting it crush me like it had all those years ago.

"Why?"

"It was where she said she always felt safe, with me. I laid her down and she released a watery breath. She looked at me and..." It was like the chain snapped and I sobbed against Quill's chest. He held me in silence as I got it all out. "She said she loved me. Asked me to live for her, be what I had to be to make this right."

"Oh, Black." He pressed a kiss to the top of my head as I soaked his shirt with over thirty years of pent up sorrow.

"I killed him. Took me a decade, but I found him rotting in a cell. I paid a ridiculous amount of money to have them all turn their backs. I choked him with the chains he'd held Sunshine prisoner with. It was in that moment when I vowed to be what the police never could be. I was Plan B."

"B for Black," Quill spoke softly.

"Now you know why I do what I do."

He pulled my head away from his chest and I looked deep into his eyes, seeing a power I'd never seen radiate from this beautiful man before me. "I never needed to know."

I wanted to see his green eyes so badly in that moment. "Can you take your contacts out? I want to see you."

He sat back slightly, but never removed himself from my lap, and I watched as he plucked the white contacts out of his eyes and wrapped them in a tissue he had in his pocket.

"You just ruined them."

He shrugged. "Your request was more important than stupid contacts."

We stared at each other silently for a minute and I half blurted out but wholly meant it, "I'm going to kiss you, Quill."

His smile was wide and brilliant. "I'm going to let you, Terrance."

Chapter Twenty-Two

Quill

A part of me felt so conflicted inside. I wanted Black more than I had ever wanted any other person in my entire life, but I wasn't sure this was the right timing. We had evaded explosions and Black had told me the most heartbreaking story I'd ever heard, which had some odd parallels to my own life. I didn't know if Black wanted me because he saw a reflection of Sunshine, needed comfort, or truly wanted me. But the rest of me didn't care. Black wanted me and I was going to let him have me.

The feel of Black's big hand cupping the back of my head, pulling me toward his lips, was almost surreal. I'd thought so much about him to the point I questioned if I was obsessed. I didn't want to embarrass myself, but the need to feel as much of him as he'd let me was all consuming. And I went willingly mouth-first into my fairytale.

Bourbon and Black assaulted my senses as hungry mouths and eager tongues collided in a ravenous kiss that never ended. I barely felt Black lift me, his hands gripping my ass. He was walking us somewhere, I didn't know, didn't care. I'd go to the ends of the earth and plunge into Hell for this man at this moment.

Then I was falling, and a rush of cold encompassed me as we separated. My nerves were squashed and Black hovered over me, smiling.

"Don't be afraid, I won't hurt you, Quill. I just wanted you in my bed."

Don't be afraid. I spent my life around men who only made me feel fear. Like walking on eggshells was the only way to move. With the snap of his fingers, Black could make them all disappear. His power was immeasurable. I could be snuffed from this world at his request and no one would ever know. And none of that mattered, because I wasn't afraid of him. I felt safe.

When Black removed his shirt, I froze. His skin glistened with passion's sweat, there were ripples and curves that showed how hard he worked at sculpting his body, but it was the tattoo across his chest that had me mesmerized. Wings.

"Angel?" I questioned as my fingers grazed over the ink.

"Phoenix." His intense eyes bore into mine.

"You rose again?"

He shook his head. "I'm always rising."

He didn't wear his memories on his back where they could hide and be forgotten, they were front and center. Reminding him that from these ashes, he will always rise.

"It's amazing, you're amazing."

The side of his mouth rose, and all conversation ended when he removed his pants. There he was like a perfect giant. Energy, power, sex, and passion pulsated over his naked body. He was art, and the unworthiness returned.

"What was that?" he asked as he knelt on the bed, so close I could feel his heat, smell his scent.

"Nothing, just…" I shook my head and feigned a smile. "You're hotter than I thought you'd be."

With narrowed eyes, Black once again crawled over me. "I'm pushing fifty, Quill. In a few years, I will be over the hill and you'll still be in your twenties. When I looked at you all these months, I saw a kid. Someone too young to know shit. But you know more than most. You're stunning, and while you look at me and see a God, I look at you and see an angel. An untouchable angel I shouldn't want but do. Don't feel unworthy, feel appreciated."

Like I was precious, Black removed each piece of my clothing with frustrating slowness. I wanted to jump him at the same time I was enjoying this odd tenderness I'd never experienced before. When he got to my legs, he slid my silky pants off, kissing all the way down to the ankle. I would have wept with the kindness he showed me if I wasn't so fucking horny.

"You usually wear black bracelets." His fingers touched over the silver bangles on my wrist as they rested across my abdomen. My legs slid on either side of him and his incredible body inched even closer.

"Yes," I gasped, unable to say many words at all.

"There's a story there?" He arched an eyebrow and I knew he'd discover everything. So, I slid them off and tossed them to the side. I raised my arms where faint lines adorned both sides.

A storm raged in his silver eyes, one of anger, protectiveness. The lion that rippled beneath his surface looked ready to roar.

"It was right after my father died. My world felt suffocating. The loneliness slammed into me daily after seeing how my mom was disappearing before my eyes and how my brother was. Well, I saw a video on YouTube. Some guy said it released his demons, the darkness in his veins, and he could feel something other than the sadness, the forever loneliness that was drowning him."

Black gently rubbed his pointer over the lines. "Did it?"

I shook my head. "I did it the first time and just felt pain. I wasn't a fan of pain. So, I thought I did it wrong. I did it a few more times, but no. My brother saw them once and told me I was such a failure, I couldn't even kill myself right, and then I was shown a different kind of torture."

Black covered my body with his, his arms on both sides of my head, cradling me in a safe, secure, and fucking hot cocoon.

"I'm sorry you've felt so much pain. I'm sorry no one saved you."

"You did." His eyebrows were bushy but sculpted, blond with a few silver streaks. I wanted to feel them, so I did.

"I didn't save you, not yet. But I will figure this all out. When it's over, you will be free."

Be free. It was an odd thing to say. "And you?"

He tilted his head. "Me?"

"Will I be free of you or will what's about to happen here end here?"

He stared at me, unspoken words saying so much.

"Let's get through tonight then, shall we?" I tried to wiggle, but his weight was too much, so I wrapped my legs around him. "If I only get tonight, then you best be rockin' my world."

He leaned in, taking my lips in a searing kiss. His tongue slid over my teeth and I could've come right there from his kiss alone. When breathing became an issue, he eased down to my neck, licking and sucking, eliciting moans that sounded inhuman. It felt like my body was firing synapses through my brain and body. I had never felt such electricity.

"God, Black, your mouth."

When he was at the juncture of my leg and cock, he gave me a sensuous look. *Could you die from an orgasm?* I thought it was possible, because I wasn't sure I'd get through this alive.

When he took my cock in his mouth, I thought death was imminent. When the suction surrounding my hardened flesh became almost too much, I might have screamed, "I'm dying."

"No, no, no, you're not dying tonight. Not even a little bit." He winked, then sat back just enough to lift my legs so my knees were on the sides of my head. Before I could say another word, his mouth was on my hole. Tongue, teeth, and lips. *What the fuck?* No one had ever rimmed me, or cared much about my pleasure like Black was. I wanted him inside me so badly, I yanked on his hair until he lifted off me.

"You have to fuck me, now!" Even I heard the plea in my own words. Gently, he put my legs down and reached over me to the bedside drawer.

He grabbed lube and a condom, and the butterflies in my belly were full on breakdancing.

My heartbeat was so loud, I wouldn't be able to hear a word Black said. But he seemed in the same trance. His cock jutted out, the tip glistening with pre-come I was desperate to taste. I made a mental note to wake him with an extraordinary blow job in the morning. I would taste this man before the fairytale ended.

He pressed his slippery finger in and I arched up the bed. "No, you, your cock. I'm good, just fuck me."

His chuckle vibrated over my skin, and I wanted to weep and cheer when he removed his finger and placed the condom on his *holy-shit-that's-huge* cock.

I took a deep breath as he covered me once more. He lifted my leg over his shoulder, and when he kissed me, I floated. Black was everywhere, his tongue in my mouth, his fingers in my hair, and with a thrust, his cock was buried deep. I didn't feel like just me, I felt like a we. Us.

There was no pounding, no wham bam, thank you ma'am from Black. Force was what I knew, and I felt the tear roll down the side of my face at the realization Black was rocking my world by cherishing me with each pump, each kiss, and each caress. He gave me something I'd never had in my entire adult life. He gave me love's truth. The truth was we, I, mattered, I was a gift. There was an overwhelming wave that poured over me in the moment when when my orgasm rushed through me. I wanted to beg it to stop, I wasn't ready to let go. I wanted so much more. More than I had never wished for before.

Black didn't jump off me after he climaxed. He kissed me, wiped away my tears, and never questioned why they were there in the first place. Not because he didn't care, but because he did. I knew how much trouble I was in because I could fall hard for Terrance Black, but I feared he'd never let himself love again.

Chapter Twenty-Three

Black

I woke to an incredible suction around my morning wood and a pleasant humming that was felt straight up my spine.

"Mmm. This is my favorite way to wake up." I saw the shape of Quill's head under the sheet and lightly rubbed over it.

Reaching orgasm wouldn't take long, I was always hard as steel in the morning, and with Quill's body wrapped around mine all night, it was like an all-night edging.

Quill's fingers scraped my inner thighs until he was cupping my balls and pushing me right over the edge. He moaned as he swallowed my come, and I was shocked my dick was already twitching back to hardness.

"I knew it," Quill said as he peeked out of the covers, arms crossed over my chest and a sappy smile on his angelic face.

"What's that?"

"You'd taste amazing."

Yep, dick definitely wanted more. But the shrill of my cell phone popped our lustful bubble and the reality of why Quill was here in the first place came crashing down.

"Black," I spoke into the phone, watching carefully as Quill slipped off me and to the side. He watched my face, likely searching for my reaction to what the Team X leader was saying to me. He'd get none.

"Morning, sir. Sorry there was nothing to report until now, but we have been able to get a lead on the bombings." He was speaking fast but clearly, and whatever room he was in made his voice reverberate.

"That's fine. I was busy myself last night as well." I shot a wink at Quill, glad when I got a little smile out of him.

"Very good, anything about the case?"

"No. Tell me your findings."

"Right, so. Three cars exploded outside Joker's Sin. Fortunately, only one person was injured but will make a full recovery. The placement of the bombs didn't seem like they were made to kill anyone."

Interesting conclusion. "Why do you believe that?"

"Two were in the alley beside Joker's Sin, minimal if any traffic. The other was an abandoned vehicle that was next to a vacant building across from Joker's Sin. Also, low traffic."

"And you think what?"

He cleared his throat. "We don't think anything, sir, we know. This was to scare, not kill."

At the club, Quill had asked if it was Ronnie, and we were all quick to tell him absolutely not. But maybe he was involved somehow.

"Do we have a who?"

Quill slid out of bed, and I watched as his stunning body, all legs and smooth skin, walked into the bathroom.

"No fingerprints have been recovered. The cameras around Joker's Sin caught a man in a hoodie go down the alley and back over to the abandoned car, so we suspect that's the guy."

The Sterlings could have hired someone to scare Quill into dropping the charges and go away.

"We need that video."

"Already obtained, sir. Would you like someone to send it your way or do you want to come in?"

A part of me very much wanted to view it here, but I wasn't sure I was ready for Quill to see it. "I'll come down to the office. I need three guys here to watch Quill."

"Done, sir."

"I'll be there in a couple of hours. Let me get ready and as soon as the guys get here, I'll head over."

After I hung up, I grabbed a pair of briefs and slipped them on. I passed the bathroom where it sounded like Quill was showering. I had a huge urge to join him, but I knew I'd never leave if I did. Instead, I opted to make coffee and cook something for breakfast.

The shower turned off just as the last of the coffee dripped into the carafe. By the time Quill joined me in the kitchen, I had some eggs and bacon on a plate for him.

"You cook?" His eyes widened as he took in the meal.

"Yes. I like surviving," I chuckled, and poured him a mug of coffee. "How do you take your coffee?"

"Ahh, and the barista becomes the patron." He pursed his lips as he took in the items on the counter. "Two scoops of sugar and some caramel milk please."

I slid the mug to him and we were silent for a few minutes before he spoke again.

"So, what's the dilly, they catch the guy?"

"Dilly?" What the fuck?

He rolled his eyes as he took a sip of coffee. "The deal, the situation."

I nodded even though I didn't understand the lingo. "Right. Well, I have to go into the office. Three guys are coming to stay here until I return. Hopefully, we can figure this all out quickly and you can return home."

Quill's eyes scanned my large kitchen. It was an open plan, so they stopped when his gaze hit the window across the way in the living room. The view was vast and gorgeous. You could see the mountains that were barren since the leaves had all fallen. The branches all looked like they were reaching for the sky or paying homage to Hart Castle many miles away.

"What is it?" I asked, concerned by his pained expression.

"Am I going to have babysitters for the rest of my life?"

"No." I cleared our dishes and when I walked back to him, he gave me a pleading look, wanting more than my taciturn answer.

"This will end. Like I said last night, you'll be free of all this and won't have to worry…" My mind went to the hooded guy.

"That." He pointed an accusing finger at me. "That face, what did you just think about?"

I didn't want to upset Quill, but at the same time, keeping anything from him could inadvertently put him in more danger.

"There was a video of the guy who might have planted the bombs. My team thinks it was a scare tactic. That the guy was hired."

Quill nodded as his fingers fiddled with his silver bracelets. "Scare me into dropping the charges? That's what you're thinking, isn't it?"

"Most likely. My attorney informed me this morning that the restraining order was granted and has been delivered. My guess? That was the final straw for the Sterlings. You were granted the temporary ex parte, which is fourteen days. He will have to go to court and fight it and if he loses, it will stay with him. If your charges stick and he goes to trial and he loses, forget it, he's done."

"So, it is Ronnie then?"

Brushing a stray hair that covered one of his green eyes, I answered, "It's probable he or his father hired someone to scare you, yes."

"I wanted to drop them."

The clock said I had a few extra minutes, so I sat beside him. "I know, and you know now what I think about the authorities. Nothing may come of this, but it will be public record and will taint their family name. I think Bartholomew Sterling fears that more than anything. Whether his son evades persecution or not, their name is tarnished."

"That's the thing." He turned in his seat and our knees just touched. "Your hate the police, which I totally get. Why do it this way, why not do it your way?"

The faint thud of an oncoming headache was beckoning me. "People like the Sterlings don't just disappear. I would if I had to, but I hoped this would be enough. I'm starting to think I need a new, better plan."

"But it's not enough. So what, I hide here until it's over? And what happens if Ronnie does face justice and their name is smudged? I won't be free, Black, they will want revenge. That hooded guy will come for me, mark my words."

There was something in Quill's tone, almost like he knew who the hooded guy was, and I wanted to ask but the clock indicated I didn't have time.

"Can we talk more about this later? I have to get ready. Three people are coming here. Don't give them a hard time, please?"

A tiny lift coupled with a mischievous glint in his eyes told me Quill was going to ask for something.

"Okay… on one condition."

And there was that headache. "What?"

He waved his hand over the room. "Can I make this place look like Christmas?"

Christmas? "What did you have in mind?"

"Tree, just a little holiday cheer. Please?" *He batted his eyes, fucking batted them, and oh for fuck's sake, is he jutting his lip out?*

"Fine, but they get the supplies. You stay here!"

He nodded excitedly and hopped off the chair. "I'm going to make a list. Oh, and a credit card, please."

What the hell had I agreed to?

Chapter Twenty-Four

Quill

"Okay, Steve, I need a tree. One that's not so big it hits the ceiling because the star has to go there." He shook his head, but was on the phone handling that, which made me turn to Leo.

"Lights, garland, ornaments. Some stockings, you know, make it look like Santa's workshop."

Leo's dark eyes narrowed. "Mr. Black okayed all this?"

"Indeedy doo, now please hurry, I want this almost done by the time he gets home."

He said he'd be back, and now it was Jaclyn's turn. She smiled brightly and I was glad someone was happy to be a part of Operation Christmas Extravaganza.

"While I want to bake, I want the smell of Christmas more. There is this new place on Fifth called Vayne. Can you see if they have bakery things and like, Christmas hams or whatever?"

"Absolutely. I think this is a great idea. Mr. Black is going to be really surprised."

I just hoped it was a good surprise.

I cleaned the entire place while I waited for everyone and everything. It was already pretty great, but I found pine scented cleaner and thought it would make the place smell perfect.

"Tree," Steve said as two huge, burly men carried in the super big tree. Good thing Black had cathedral ceilings. Jaclyn slipped the stand on, and when the tree was secure, she filled it with water and we got the skirt on.

"I love it. Perfect job, guys." With a few grunts, they left, and then Leo brought in boxes of decorations and such.

"Where'd you get all that?" Jaclyn asked.

"Lana took care of it, Roger just drove it over."

If Lana was in charge, I knew these were going to be awesome decorations. It only took fifteen minutes of them all watching me struggle for them to help me with lights, garland, and decorations. By the time the tree was done, Jaclyn announced the food delivery.

I darted into the kitchen, making sure the counters were clear.

"Someone order Christmas?" the voice asked. When the box was lowered, I saw it was that Xander guy from the ball.

"Oh, hey, you're the owner of Vayne."

The blush that painted his cheeks was adorable. "Guilty."

"I thought your food was so outstanding. I knew you'd be able to help me pull this off."

He scanned the place, eyes going to the top of the tree.

"What are you trying to pull off, exactly?"

"Christmas, of course." I began removing items from the box. Ham, mashed potatoes, corn, bread, cookies, so much Christmas.

"You live here?" Xander asked, and where I once found that question to be benign, it now made me skeptical.

"Um… no, it's not my place."

He nodded, hands in his back pockets and not showing any indication he was leaving. Steve and Leo were eyeing him, likely wondering why he was still here. The food was purchased over the phone and paid for.

"It's gorgeous. Oh wow." He ran over to the wall of windows where Hart Castle stood. The sun had set and it was lit up beautifully. Christmas lights and everything. I certainly wouldn't want to be the person decorating that place.

"Amazing view, huh?" I followed, leaving enough distance between me and him. Jaclyn was sitting on a love seat by the tree, pretending to be reading a magazine.

He practically had his nose pressed to the glass. "A million-dollar view for sure. Wow!"

I returned to the kitchen and watched him, a big smile and shining wonderment filled his expression. I was sure Black's people were going to shit a brick, but I felt like the guy wasn't ready to leave.

"Do you want to maybe help me set all this food up?"

As predicted, Jaclyn, Leo, and Steve all turned their attention to me, their gazes rivaling the crackling fire.

"I'd love to." Xander walked with a bounce in his step and when he picked up the chef's knife to cut the ham, I thought the three bodyguards were going to have a heart attack.

For the next hour, Xander helped me set up the food and desserts to look magazine quality and I was so grateful. He wasn't a bad guy, it seemed like maybe he was just lonely.

"Thanks for helping me. I can cook to live, but nothing this amazing."

Again, Xander blushed and maybe another time I would've flirted, but the thought of Black and last night filled my mind and nothing else compared.

"Anytime, uh…" He looked up. Jaclyn was sitting on the stool by the breakfast bar, Leo was scanning the view, and Steve was pacing, giving less than warm glares at the two of us. "Are these guys your friends?"

I chuckled as his eyes followed Black's people's movements. "No, they work for the owner here. I'm just crashing while my place is being painted." The lie fell from my mouth like butter. Jaclyn's eyebrows raised and I gave her a "hush it" expression.

"I see. Well, do you ever do the meditation thing at Fredrick's Park?" he continued, perfecting the garnish as he spoke.

"No, what's that?"

"It's three times a week, I believe. Um, if you have a number,

I can text you the schedule. I go to the park a lot, I've seen it and I've been thinking of going to it, but…"

I knew he was going to say he had no one to go with and while I didn't want him thinking it was a date, I sort of wanted to wash that uncertain look he had going on.

"Sure, I'll put it in your phone and just message me and we can totally work it out. Never can have too many friends, right?"

He handed his phone over, mumbling something I couldn't quite make out. I texted myself from his phone and he smiled when it came through. *Did he think I'd put a fake number in?*

After Xander left, I quickly took another shower. I couldn't wear these clothes again, so I hunted around Black's room. There were pants and shirts, but all I'd swim in and could likely rival Oliver Twist asking Mr. Bumble, "Please, Sir, I want some more." I did want more Black, but I didn't need Black coming up with excuses not to be with me with the reminder of my age and stature.

With a towel around my hips, I called out for Jaclyn. She came in, eyes widening when she saw me.

"I have nothing to wear. I can't wear his clothes, and nothing here comes close."

She chuckled and said she'd be right back. I waited ten minutes, but she did indeed return.

"Here. My partner, Jane, hope you don't mind, but she had some sweat pants and a Spiderman t-shirt in my trunk."

It was perfect. "I don't care whose they are. If they fit, I'm happy."

After she left me to it, I changed and brushed my teeth with a spare toothbrush I'd found this morning. I felt better and ready to jingle Black's balls when he returned.

Chapter Twenty-Five

Black

I watched the tape for what felt like twenty times. Not once did the guy- and I was sure it was a guy- look up, to the left, anything. He knew what he was doing. He was precise and fast. I wanted so badly to pass this off to Lee to see what he could come up with, but I had to stand my ground with him. They had shit to work out.

"Do we even have a reflection from a car window or the pole or anything?" I asked, my fingers burning as I clenched them. I didn't like all this mystery, especially since it was a dangerous game this douche was playing.

"None, sir. We thought we had one when he went to the abandoned car, but it seems like he was wearing one of those mouth masks. Skiers use them."

So, if the Sterlings hired this person, and I had a feeling they had, he wasn't stupid.

"Sir," my guy began. "Maybe Quill can recognize him from his build."

"Why would you even suggest he see this?" Rage simmered just below the surface at his suggestion. "He doesn't need to see the lengths someone went through to terrify him."

"Sir, before Lee went on sabbatical, he gave me Quill's file. I went through it and continued where he left off."

I swiveled in my chair, wondering what more was found that Lee hadn't. Fear and anger intertwined in my gut. "Go on."

"One main concern Lee had was the brother. He comes in and out of Quill's life. Takes his money and leaves him in the hospital. Quill's been evading him, and judging by Dylan's history, it probably enrages him. If he needs money and the Sterlings are offering, and in exchange he can seek a little revenge on Quill, he'd take it."

The realization hit me like a freight train, of course. I agreed to take it back to my house and show it to Quill. I had been at the office all day and the sun had set a few hours ago. Jaclyn had called me earlier, saying she couldn't promise Leo or Steve wouldn't shoot Quill if he didn't stop with the tinsel time happy hour.

A smile tugged at my lips as I could very easily seeing a Christmas fueled Quill in my head. He had an elven quality about him for sure. Give the kid some green and red tights, a hat, and a candy cane, and he'd be the hottest elf ever.

The familiar doubt that periodically hibernated in the back of my mind reared its ugly head. I had given into my urges with Quill, but there was no way we would ever be permanent. I was too old, he was too young, and our lives would be constantly on the cusp of violence. When this was done and Quill was safe, I wanted him to never worry about violence again.

"Black," Lana's voice called as I was walking through the lobby to my waiting car.

"Hi, Lana. Before you ask, Quill is fine, he's safe."

She smiled but shook her head. "I knew he was. I was asking about the Christmas Ball, the one we're supposed to go to on Friday."

Shit. I had forgotten about that; she was so happy to have been asked and I knew even if this wasn't resolved with Quill, I'd have people able to watch him.

"Of course. I will be at your place at seven, does that work?"

She bit her lip, uncertainty painting a picture I was familiar with when it came to Lana.

"You're so busy, and with Quill, I understand if you…"

I rested my hand on her shoulder, then smiled softly, knowing how hard it was for Lana to be confident.

"Hush. I will handle everything. It'll be a lovely evening."

I made sure she made it to her car before I slipped into the back of mine. Resting my head on the seat, I replayed the night before with Quill. The suddenness of it all. One minute, I was telling him to stop flirting and repeating the word no, the next, there was an explosion and a need to be as close to him as humanly possible. Lana often said I needed therapy, but I didn't think there was a therapist alive who could handle my nightmare of a psychosis.

The drive back to my house was fairly uneventful, an email from Poe in regard to getting entrance into the Vaults was met with a short response:

Mr. Black,

Mr. Hart understands your concern to check into the Sterlings history and such, but unless you can give him a better reason than you think he may be violent, I'm afraid your request is denied. Have a good evening.

Poe.

When Bill and Mace needed to get into the vault, there were no snags. Granted, Zagan was a vicious man and the town was almost a warzone because of that situation. When I reached out to Poe, the car bombs hadn't happened yet, so I shot off another email explaining my thoughts on the current situation.

The car dipped and I realized we were in my garage, so I slipped my phone in my pocket and stepped out when the car stopped.

"Have a good evening, sir," the driver said as he went left and I went right.

My mind wouldn't slow down, wondering what Quill had done all day. Something ridiculous I was sure if Leo and Steve wanted to hang him by the garland.

When the elevator door opened, the scent of pine and the sound of Snoopy and The Red Baron assaulted my senses.

Leo quirked a brow as he leaned against the wall adjacent to the elevator.

"Have a fun day?" I chuckled when he rolled his eyes.

"I'm walking the perimeter. I can't deal with this anymore." We switched places and he went downstairs and I went forward toward the Christmas explosion.

"Merry Christmas!" Quill shouted as he stood beside a huge tree decorated to the top. The entire place was transformed and the smells that permeated the air took me back to my childhood.

"Wow." I scanned the room. Stockings, garland, and lights. "You went all out."

"I did! It's not often someone hands me their credit card and lets me decorate their gorgeous home." His toe scuffed the hardwood floor and while his face was all smiles, his posture showed his nerves. He was worried I'd hate it, and I was sure Steve and Leo had done nothing to make him think otherwise. Jaclyn, at least, was smiling by the window and I was glad she was on his side.

"It's amazing, thank you. I don't get much time to decorate and I don't want to hire a stranger to come into my space and get it ready for whatever holiday is forthcoming." I took a few steps toward him, intent on kissing his bubble gum tinted lips, when my stomach growled.

"Hungry?" Quill ran toward the kitchen. Following his direction, I saw a spread worthy of a ball.

"Holy shit."

"Yeah, I got a lot, but leftovers are the best and with all the protection you seem to always have around you, your guys… and girls," he winked at Jaclyn, "could eat."

"So thoughtful of you." I couldn't stop my feet if I tried.

Suddenly, I was towering over him, cupping his cheek and pressing my lips to his.

His tongue delved into my mouth and when his arms reached up, barely wrapping around my neck, I scooped him up, moaning when his legs circled my waist.

"Sir?" Jaclyn's voice interrupted us. "I am terribly sorry to interrupt, but Leo is asking what the evening plans are to be?"

I turned my head, trying to keep my composure as Quill took my earlobe in his mouth, teeth nibbling enough to sting perfectly.

"Have Leo and Steve come here. You as well, eat, and we need to talk about a few things."

That seemed to jolt Quill out of his sexual ministrations to ask, "You found something, didn't you?"

"Let's eat, please. We can talk after."

I was glad he didn't argue with me and soon the room was filled with people fixing their plates and heading to the dining table.

No one spoke aside from commenting on how delicious the food was and after all the dishes were cleared away, I called everyone to the living room where I was setting up my laptop to link with my television.

"Quill," I said, causing him to stop mid-sit on the couch, staring at me with a flicker of concern. "We have video of the person who set up the bombs and they appear to be very smart. No one can make him out, but since this seems to be directed toward you, we wondered if you could tell who they were."

He nodded, sat on the couch Indian-style, and began fidgeting with his thumbs. I hated his fear, but he had to see. We had to know.

The television came to life, not much to see at first, passersby and such. The screen was cut in half, one camera on the alley, the other pointed in the direction of the abandoned car. We were able to cut out nonsense shots so Quill could see the person well enough.

A minute later, the hooded man came on the screen. There was no reaction from Quill other than a cock of his head and the narrowing of his eyes.

The alley was poorly lit, so I wasn't surprised when he said nothing there. When the person got to the abandoned car, it only took a second before his gasp filled the room.

"You recognize them?" Jaclyn asked.

"I… go back a few seconds and freeze it when he rests his left arm on the hood."

I did as he asked and instead of watching the TV, I watched him. There was recognition, fear, and some anger in his gaze.

"That's my brother." His voice was so soft, but in the quiet of the room, we all heard it.

"You're sure?" I asked, trying to see what made Quill come to that conclusion.

He got off the couch and walked to the screen. He pointed to the bomber's forearm where the hoodie sleeve was pushed up.

"That tattoo, you only see part of it, but if he lifted it all the way up, you'd see a scorpion spearing a snake." He sighed, "That's Dylan."

Now I needed to figure out if Dylan was a separate problem or if the Sterlings were using him like we seemed to think.

CHAPTER TWENTY-SIX

Quill

I left the living room shortly after discovering it was my brother behind the car bombs. I think a part of me sort of knew with all the cloak and dagger shit Black was spouting earlier, but I had hoped I was wrong.

He went on that it was a scare tactic most likely, but I knew Dylan. I was hiding from him, and I knew at some point, he'd get tired of my hide and seek and just end it all.

Jaclyn, Leo, and Steve were sitting and talking to Black about the next step in their plan, so I excused myself to put all the leftovers away in the fridge. I could still hear them formulating plans since it was an open concept house, but I pretended to be in a safe bubble in my head.

"Quill," Black's voice called out, and I turned in his direction. "I know you're upset." Understatement. "But if you could give us a profile of your brother the best you can, it may better help us understand his motivation."

Motivation? When did Black become creepy Doctor Loomis here? I slammed the refrigerator door and stormed into the room. Black's eyes widened a fraction, probably from not expecting my anger, but I was livid. Why couldn't people leave me alone?

"You want his motivation?" I asked, using air quotes. "Great, okay. Dylan is a fucking psychopath. When he was five, he got joy in burning the legs off spiders. Whenever my parents weren't looking, he liked to smack me, lock me in a closet, and tell them I went to a friend's house, leaving me there for hours. After my dad died, he got worse. He beat me, took my money, and dropped me at the doors of whatever ER we were near. His motivation is pain and money. He likes to inflict the hurt and take the dough."

Jaclyn found something on her lap fascinating, and Steve and Leo stared at me like I was crazy. Black, on the other hand, slammed the folder he had open down on the glass table.

"Your brother is shitty. He did fucked up shit and is going to continue unless we stop him." He shot up and took three steps, putting him directly in front of me. "Now, I think the Sterlings found him, hired him, and he's doing the whole 'two birds, one stone' thing. I have a plan, though."

A plan? "And what's that, tough guy?" I couldn't help my defiance, but confliction was poking all sorts of holes through my mind.

"I think the Sterlings are scaring you to drop the charges so as not to taint their good name."

"Right, we know that. You want me to drop them?"

He shook his head. "No, you're not dropping them. I have no use for justice in this city, but it's something that bothers them, and you being hidden will frustrate them the closer we get to the hearing date." He lifted my chin with his finger, silver eyes glinting against the roaring fire ablaze beside us. "Nothing happens to you, but I need them scared, angry, and annoyed. It's then they will make a mistake. I can't just go in their home and off them all, it would raise too many flags and hurt my standing with the Hart family."

"You have standing with them?"

"I know they aren't pissed at me, and I know they have a power that keeps this city alive. The heir has his finger on the pulse of Haven Hart, and I don't need them cutting my cord to balance shit. I need to be the balance."

I didn't understand what a lot of that meant, but Black was an enigma to me and he only shared what he wanted to, even though he had shared so much with me. Truth of it was, we all had secrets and we'd all die with a few unspoken.

"What's your plan?"

"I will use a decoy. My car will drop them, meaning you, off at the apartment where they will keep their head down, so hopefully, your brother or whoever will show up and we will grab them. One Sterling or your brother disappearing for a while won't be an issue. But it's the best idea right now." He released my chin and rubbed the bridge of his nose. "You have to trust me."

"I never trust anyone completely." I spoke on reflex, because it was true. "But I trust you more than anyone else."

"Okay. Good." We both seemed to be stuck in some sort of trance until one of the guys cleared his throat.

"Ginger is close to Quill's size, maybe an inch taller, but it won't be noticeable. We'd just need to dye his hair. What color is that?" Leo asked.

"Gunmetal gray. I can write the brand and such down for you."

Black nodded and asked Steve to have Ginger come here tomorrow morning.

"That's all for tonight. You three are free to go. Your replacements are outside and keeping an eye out. I don't need internal protection while I'm here."

They bid us goodnight and when they all left, a wave of awkwardness swept over the room.

"So," I said. "What happens if someone takes a shot at Ginger, thinking it's me, and he dies?"

Black whipped his head around and his braid flew from his back over to his shoulder.

"You can't worry about such things. Every person who works for me whether in security or other knows the risks."

"They're expendable?" I leaned against the counter hoping it masked the shaking in my legs.

"They're necessary." He gave me a narrowed look as his gaze went to my legs. "Bath, let's go."

He walked down the hallway toward the bedroom and... *did he just order me?*

"Hey," I shouted. "Are you telling me what to do?" I followed him down, wanting to maybe stop him.

"I did." He was removing his watch when I entered.

"You're not my dad or..."

His laughter filled the room and when he met my eyes, they were smiling.

"If I'm not mistaken, you wanted me to be your daddy."

Oh... OH!

Excitement filled my veins. "Are we roleplaying?" I rubbed my hands with glee.

"No." He went into the en-suite and a second later, the water started.

"So, what are we doing then?" I stood in the door frame, salivating as Black removed his clothes and pulled the tie out of his hair.

"Taking a bath, Quill. This isn't a difficult concept. People have been doing it since 1883."

Black started the bath, poured in some bubble bath, and soon enough, the bathroom filled with the scent of vanilla and sandalwood. "How do you know that?"

"I know things." He waggled his eyebrows as his gloriously naked form slipped into the tub.

I had never removed my clothes so fast, I practically fell into the tub.

"Easy there," Black rumbled against my neck as he steadied me.

The water felt amazing and I rested my head on Black's chest. The rise and fall of his chest lulled me into a calmer state. The steam from the tub sent a relaxing aroma all around me and I could've fallen asleep. I almost did.

"Hey." Black's lips grazed over my heated skin, causing goosebumps to break free.

"Hey."

"Let's get some sleep. Ginger will be here in the morning and we need to be rested."

Bed? Sleep? "Wait." I spun in the water, pressing my hands against his chest. "We aren't going to have sex? I thought that's what this was all about, the tubbing and smelly bubbles and things."

He chuckled, and damn if he wasn't hotter when he smiled. "Sometimes it's okay to be taken care of, Quill. Not everything ends with sex."

"What? But..."

He rose from the water and I watched as streams ran down the contours of his muscles and crevices. He opened a large, white, fluffy towel for me, brows raised as he waited patiently. I covered myself up and observed Black's hair routine.

I was mesmerized as I watched Black putting stuff in his hair, brushing it, and blow drying it. I stood there wrapped in the warm towel, unable to move. He did it all completely naked. His routine felt like a secret, like I was privy to seeing a side of him no one else was able to see.

"Friday, I am taking Lana to that Christmas ball I promised. She was nice enough to remind me of that today when I saw her. I will have plenty of protection for you, so there won't be any worries." Black spoke while he slipped on a pair of dark-gray briefs.

"Friday. That's the day after tomorrow. If Ginger does his thing tomorrow and it all goes well, I may be fine on my own, no?" I wrapped the towel around my waist and realized I had no clean clothes. The white outfit I wore at Joker's Sin was a mess now and the outfit Jaclyn had given me, well, I didn't want to put it back on.

"Even if this goes well and they approach Ginger tomorrow or even early the following day, it will not be settled and I'd feel better if you were still under protection." When he put his hands on his hips, his stance was imposing. My stomach clenched with lust and a little bit of fear.

"Well, I'm out of clothes." I gestured to the crumpled pile on the floor. "Jaclyn had those in her car, but now I have nothing."

He eyed the pile and I had to admit, it was adorable seeing the realization that clean clothes had completely escaped his mind.

"Shit, I'm sorry. Okay. I will get you some clothes tomorrow. Even if you're still here, you'll have clean things."

I ripped the towel from my body and struck what I hoped was a sexy pose. "I guess I'm wearing my birthday suit to bed then."

With another chuckle, Black walked out of the bathroom, but not before pinching my ass.

Chapter Twenty-Seven

Black

I didn't wake up to an amazing blow job, but I did wake to an empty bed. I could hear Quill's laughter coming from the kitchen, so adorned in just my briefs, I followed the infectious sound.

"That is so great, Dr. Mason. Maybe I can come and get Lady Whiskers McMeowers today?"

Who the fuck was he talking to and who the hell was McDonalds Whiskey what?

He laughed loudly just as I rounded the corner. His back was to me and he had a sheet wrapped around his body. "I can't figure out a better name for her. I liked them all, so I mashed them."

Her?

"Thank you, oh, can you tell me the final cost of her medical bill?"

Medical bill? Oh, this is his cat.

"Eep. Okay, thanks, Doc."

I observed him a minute before making my presence known. After he placed his cell down, his shoulders hunched and he rested his face in his hands. I knew defeat when I saw it.

"Lady Whiskers McMeowers?" I spoke as softly as I could, but he jumped all the same.

"Shit, you scared me." He spun around and the blanket slipped off his shoulders, exposing his gorgeous skin.

"Your cat?" He nodded. "I'm guessing the bill is high?"

"Yeah, it's ridiculous dollars and insanity cents."

I had a dog growing up and when he broke his leg, it cost my folks three thousand dollars. Animals were costly.

"You have to pick her up today?"

He slid from the stool and wrapped the sheet tighter. "Yeah, if I don't they are going to likely charge me to board her and I can barely afford the bill as is." He looked down at himself. "So, I need some clothes and if you're not cool with a cat here, then I need to go elsewhere."

I wasn't a cat person, but I seemed to seriously be a Quill person. "It's fine, when we get your clothes, we can grab a litter box and some food."

I was growing to adore his smile. "Oh, I have all that stuff at my apartment if someone can just…"

"No. The next time anyone goes to your place, it will be Ginger. Until then, no one can go there. Lana will get you clothes and I will just ask her to get a few things for her majesty McPurrfect."

He chuckled. "I'm going to have to add on to her name."

"Of course you are."

Our morning consisted of Quill calling Atlas to tell him he was going to be out for a few days. Fortunately, he wasn't met with anger. Then he called Mel and told her way too much. I explained the less they knew the better, but he explained that Mel knew the situation with Ronnie and should know that Dylan was in town in case he showed up there.

As he told Mel the details, my fingers itched to get a grip on that son of a bitch *and* the Sterlings. The vibration of my cellphone snapped me out of my rage. Lana was on her way in with clothes and cat things.

I closed the bedroom door to give him privacy and greeted Lana.

"Wow, this place looks like a Christmas wonderland." Her eyes twinkled as she took in all the décor.

"Yes, I left Quill alone for a few minutes and this happened."

She shook her head and handed me two bags. "Clothes and shoes." The third was dropped at her feet. "Cat paraphernalia."

"Thanks." I could still hear Quill on the phone in the bedroom. "I have one more favor to ask of you." Reaching in my back pocket, I handed her my credit card. "Go down to Dr. Mason's, the veterinarian, pay the bill and bring the kitten here."

Her eyes widened and I didn't need to ask her what she was thinking. I wasn't normally a soft man. Lana had seen me at my worst when Sunshine died and all the years that followed my self-destruction and the rebuild of who I was today. She knew I was beginning to care a whole lot about Quill. Every time I tried to temper it, he'd look at me, say something, or just be, and I couldn't hold back.

"Okay," her voice cracked, and if she cried, I was going to have to walk away. I wasn't answering questions or explaining myself to her or anyone. Something in my gaze must have told her that because she started walking back toward the elevator.

"Hey, did I hear someone?" Quill asked from behind me after Lana left.

"Lana, dropping off clothes and cat things." Quill raced to the clothes and sighed when he lifted a t-shirt out.

"She gets me," he said, then headed back to the bedroom to change.

After he was dressed, he began setting up everything for the royal furball and I was just answering Ginger's text to come up when Quill spoke.

"So, after Ginger leaves, we can get Her Majesty Lady Whiskers McMeowers the Purrfect?"

I stopped mid-step on my way to the elevator. "Seriously with that name?"

"Oh yeah." The waggle of his eyebrows had me chuckling just as the doors opened and Ginger stepped out.

Ginger had a small smile on his face as he observed Quill and me. "Is this an okay time?"

I worked hard at keeping my personal side apart from my professional and it wasn't that I didn't want Ginger to see me happy, I just didn't want him to see the affect Quill had on me. I righted my expression and waved him over to follow me.

"I told you to come up, did I not? Why would I say something I didn't mean?" My tone was stern, leaving no room for argument. I wasn't Ginger's friend, I was his boss and we killed people for a living.

The slight amusement faded from his pale, freckled face. "Sorry, sir."

I gestured for him to sit just as Quill came in shaking his head.

"Ahh, there's the hardass I fell in lust with." He fanned himself with his hand and dramatically fell into the wingback chair, legs dangled across the arm. "Be still my horny heart."

Like everyone else, Ginger wasn't immune to Quill's snark and bust out laughing. He tried to school his expression several times before being successful.

"If we're quite done." I gave Quill a narrowed look, but he just winked at me.

"Sir, I purchased hair dye and Lana said that she sent over a ton of clothes that are Quill's. We're close to the same height and build, so it shouldn't be an issue."

I desperately wanted to flick his nose, but I refrained. "I'm aware, Ginger, it's why Leo suggested you'd be perfect for the part." I rubbed my temples trying to keep the impending thud at bay. "Please tell me working without Jones doesn't make you stupid?"

"What?" he snapped and immediately slapped his hand over his mouth, and of course, Quill giggled.

"I'll let that slide," I said. "Jones and Lee are currently suspended."

"I'm aware, sir."

"Are you sure you can work without Jones' guidance?"

There was a challenge in those eyes of his. "I lived a long time on the streets without him. I don't need him or anyone."

That comment sucked out the last of any calm feelings. I was no one's therapist, so I just moved on. "Quill will dye your hair. He hasn't been wearing many piercings lately, so we are going to forgo anything like that, fake or otherwise. It's winter, so covering up will work perfectly from car to apartment building."

He nodded as I spoke and whatever haunted memory that showed in his eyes was now gone.

"All you have to do is go inside. If they want to get to you, they are going to either call you to leave or try and show up." I turned to Quill, who was watching us intently. "Have you received any texts or calls on your cell since the bombing?" He shook his head. "Perfect. If anyone calls him, Quill will speak. You two don't sound alike at all so if he's contacted, I will call you."

"Has anyone searched Quill's phone for whoever may have called him earlier?" Ginger asked.

"Lee is the best, but…"

Quill interrupted my sentence. "He's too stubborn to call him and ask for help."

"Stay out of my business, Quill." I hadn't spoken to Quill that way since we were at my office, and the flinch he made had me wishing I'd never said anything. I understood Quill was a free spirit of sorts, but I wasn't. Showing or telling anyone who worked for me my secrets or the depth of my emotions was a huge mistake. I couldn't afford it.

But, it wasn't Quill's fault, so I continued in a softer tone. "We know who planted the bombs, so likely, it was Quill's brother or the Sterlings."

Ginger and I went over the game plan while Quill listened,

commenting about the alarm system and asking questions about what-if scenarios. After everything was settled, Ginger went with Quill into the bathroom to dye his hair gunmetal gray. Since that was the color he had when he went into Joker's Sin, it had to be the color Ginger went with now.

I was glad Lana arrived while Ginger and Quill were in the bathroom. The kitten was somewhat pathetic looking. Gray fur, not very shiny, but Lana explained she had a special diet in the bag and antibiotics. Everything was printed out for Quill and I was grateful the cat seemed docile.

"Where did he put the litter box?" Lana asked.

"Master bathroom. But he's in there with Ginger doing hair."

Lana rolled her eyes. "Well, he was going to find out you did this for him eventually, so now is that time." With Lady Majesty puffy pants whatever the hell her name was cradled to her chest, she marched, determined, into the master bathroom.

"What the actual fuck, Lana!" Quill's voice shouted, followed by him saying, "God dammit, Black, you stubborn mule."

Chapter Twenty-Eight

Quill

I wanted to be livid with Black, first for snapping at me before with Ginger and now for him shoveling out the money for Her Majesty Lady... oh dammit, her name was too long. But as I stared at those amber eyes as Lana gently placed her in the litter box, I was just elated she was looking so much better.

"Hey there, little lady." Gently, I petted her head and she immediately rubbed her tiny face against my palm. When she meowed, my heart melted.

"That your cat?" Ginger asked as he dried his now gunmetal gray hair with a towel.

"Yeah, found her under a soggy pizza box in the alley where I work. She looked worse than she does now. I just couldn't leave her there."

My answer was met with silence. When I lifted my head, Ginger was regarding me with an expression I couldn't place.

"You don't belong in this world," he whispered to me, and a pang of hurt hit my gut.

"Excuse me?"

He shook his head like he was swishing away his thoughts. "I just mean, you live in a world where you'd rescue a cat dying under some pizza boxes and people like me and Black live in a world where the pizza boxes were there because we killed the delivery boy who was likely the cat's owner."

The pain began to burn, not a blaze of shame or guilt, but of rage. I stood, suddenly happy when Ginger stepped back. "Don't talk like you know him or me. You know what he's shown you, but not what he is." I took another step and Ginger hit the wall. "And you know zero about me. You can dig and dig and dig and never hit pay dirt when it comes to me or anyone else. Don't think you got anything figured out. What you do doesn't define who you are, Ginger."

I'd had enough. I scooped up Lady Whiskers and went to see about getting her fed.

Lana and Black were sitting on stools in the kitchen, conversing over coffee. I went toward the bag of dry and wet food and read over the directions Dr. Mason had written out for her. I was half comprehending because I was fighting with the anger that was consuming me over what Ginger had said.

"Careful opening those cans," Lana said loudly, likely trying to grab my attention. Of course, I was on the cusp of losing it and turned on her.

"Why did you feel the need to tell me that, Lana? Do I look like a fragile butterfly untainted by the real world and unable to handle a cut from a small piece of metal?" I placed the kitten on the counter when I felt her start to shake. I didn't want her to think I was angry with her. "I can handle it. I am careful, but that never matters. I get hurt anyway and just because I would have paid my last penny to save Lady doesn't mean I'm foolish, naive, or that I don't belong in your world."

I didn't know where it was all coming from, but it was like all the gas built up and the cork popped free, spilling it all everywhere.

"Okay…" Lana furrowed her brow, confusion apparent. When I dared a glance at Black, it wasn't anger I was met with, it was understanding. I hadn't expected that.

"What happened?" he asked, his approach was careful but precise. He stood in front of me. I didn't know I was clutching a can and the opener in my fists until Black tried prying them free.

"Nothing happened. I'm just... I don't know. I feel." I didn't know.

Ginger walked into the kitchen, took in the scene, and sighed.

"Quill, I didn't mean to insult you, and you weren't wrong what you said in there. I just... I don't know you or Black and you don't know me. I've never seen someone show kindness like you did in there. For a minute, my thoughts ran outta my mouth. Sorry."

Black watched Ginger, and that softness he offered me was not what he offered Ginger. He was an employee and Black liked me. It was safe to say that he showed me in the small things he was doing. But Ginger really was sorry. I could tell genuine well. Black was about to round on Ginger, so I placed a hand on his bicep to stop him.

"It's fine, Ginger. Let's not think about it. You have to get in the right headspace to go be me. So, it's all good." I nodded at Black when he gave me a questioning expression. "He better get going then."

I could tell the conversation wasn't over between Black and me.

Black kissed me softly and said he'd be back soon. I watched him go, hoping this plan worked and he stayed safe.

The plan was for Black to be in the car taking Ginger to my place. We thought it would be more believable if Black walked him to the door and said goodnight to him. Ginger had a camera on his person and of course, my apartment had video as well. Lana and I sat side by side at the dining room table, watching the four monitors showing the one in the limo, my apartment, outside my apartment, and Ginger's self-camera.

Lana and I watched the monitors. Ginger and Black talked a little in the car, but not much. There was a chasm between them, which I was happy to see. After they had left, a part of me wondered if Ginger was trying to push me away to have Black for himself. I thought he and Jones had a thing going on, which was why Jones and Lee were... oh.

"Lana, do you think Ginger is trustworthy?"

She watched the screens as she answered. "I think if Black didn't trust him, he wouldn't be doing this job right now."

"It's just... I thought Jones and Lee were a thing, but from what I was gathering, Lee was angry because Jones and Ginger were having a thing. So if Ginger was morally inclined to get between those two, wouldn't that mean he's untrustworthy?"

She took her eyes off the monitors and her gaze was stoic with a slight curve to her lips.

"Black cares for you, more than I've seen him care for anyone in a long time. Even if Ginger tried, he'd fail." She reached out and took my hand in her warm one. "As for Jones and Lee and that whole thing, those two have a complicated history we only know a fraction of. Don't compare them to you and Black."

It wasn't the right time to talk about it, so I nodded and went back to watching the monitors.

Black put on a believable show. The limo camera showed him put his hand on Ginger's lower back while whispering something in his ear, causing Ginger to chuckle. He was passable as me, but the view from the limo told me my ass was way better.

"Okay, we're at the door," Ginger said. "What now?"

"Play along."

Black leaned in and I watched, heart aching as he pressed his lips to Ginger's. The screen was muffled since the camera was on Ginger. But I heard the smacking sound.

"It means nothing, Quill," Black whispered into the microphone the moment he parted from Ginger.

Lana laughed. "He knows you."

As soon as Ginger was inside the apartment complex, Black walked back to the limo and drove off. Now we waited. Black was talking to his team as he headed back here and Lana and I couldn't take our eyes off Ginger as he slipped into the apartment and said the words that would stop the system from shooting darts at his face.

He walked around checking closets, windows, all things one should check if they wondered if someone was hiding in their place. I admitted to Lana that this was putting me to sleep and she told me to go figure out dinner since it was going to be a long night and we would need food.

I was just finishing up some spaghetti and meatballs, nothing fancy, when Black returned. I could hear his footsteps on the hardwood floor, they got louder the closer he came to the kitchen.

"Smells amazing," he said, and I'd just turned when his hulking body devoured me in an embrace and a searing kiss. His moan rumbled through me and I dropped the ladle into the sauce, splattering us in marinara.

Black's tongue lapped up the spatters on my cheek. His beard brushed against my flushed skin and he whispered, "Tastes good too."

"I sure hope you have a fire extinguisher in this place, because you're setting the house on fire with your make out session." Lana leaned against the doorframe.

"I thought you were watching the monitors?" Black spoke to her, but he made no move to separate.

"Leo is watching."

"It's a good thing I made a lot of food," I said. Black leaned down until his forehead pressed against mine and his gray eyes met my green ones.

"What are you doing to me, Quill?"

Words swam in my head of what I wanted to say, but instead, I said, "Nothing you aren't wanting me to, Black."

Chapter Twenty-Nine

Black

The entire time I was with Ginger, I hated being away from Quill. It hadn't been since Sunshine that I'd felt this way and even with her, it wasn't as strong. When I leaned into Ginger and kissed him, it was like I could feel the shot to Quill's gut.

The driver couldn't get me back to my house fast enough and as soon as the car was parked, I had to see Quill, feel and taste him.

I had asked Riordan once why he was leaving the only life he knew for another person. He told me he couldn't explain it. He said something takes over your heart and mind and suddenly, you don't know how to live without them. When he was with Teddy, breathing was easier, everything was better, and for the first time, he wanted to be a better person. I was starting to understand that now.

We all ate in front of the monitors. Ginger sat on the couch and watched TV until he passed out. Steve and Jaclyn were currently watching from a van two blocks away from Quill's place in case someone tried to make a move. There would be shifts until we got our hands on someone.

That night in bed, as Quill laid across my chest covered in sweat and come, he asked me when he could return to work and I instinctively tightened my arms around him.

"Not until this is finished."

He lifted his widened eyes to mine. "We're dealing with the Sterlings here. And my brother. This could take a while. I can't not work. I need the money."

I wanted to tell him he didn't. That I'd make sure he was financially okay. But Quill wasn't the type of person to trust a man who wanted to take care of him. His life had proved nothing came without a price, and the price generally hurt.

"You have that money you were going to pay to get your cat back, now you don't have to." It was a good solution even if Quill didn't like it and by the expression I was getting, he didn't.

"I'm giving that money to you. You paid for Lady Whiskers and you shouldn't have."

God dammit, there went my after-sex glow. "Quill, stop. I'm not taking that money from you. I don't need it and you do."

"So, we're going to have an argument?" he asked as he sat up. "Because I don't want to be naked when we do in case you make me so mad I have to storm out of the room. I doubt whoever is sitting watching the monitors would appreciate seeing me like that."

"I don't want to fight with you," I said, pushing myself up to lean against the headboard. "You're in a rush to get away from here and if you go now, it could be…" I didn't get to finish my sentence, we were interrupted by my bedroom door flying open and Nathan, my guy who was on shift watching the monitors, ran in.

"Sir, sorry to interrupt. We have a situation. Team X is on it, but it looks like someone was skulking around the complex, then climbed into an apartment window next to Quill's. That's when the team was dispatched."

Quill was wrapped in the bedsheet, but I was mostly exposed. I didn't care. I wanted to get my hands on someone who could give me answers and hopefully help end this shit. So, I pulled the sheet off me and I would've laughed when Nathan turned, banging into the wall to avoid seeing me naked.

"I'll be out in a minute. Tell whoever's on point, I want that person alive. If anyone gets gun happy and kills him, they'll be joining him."

"Yes, sir." Nathan left, leaving Quill staring at the door. I ran into the bathroom, washed up, and went to my closet.

"You're going to wear a suit?" he asked as he made his way to the bathroom.

"Yes." There was no time to explain to Quill the importance of my appearance. How intimidation was more than just actions.

As I was braiding my hair, Quill exited the bathroom fully dressed in a black t-shirt that said, "Feeling a bit stabby today." And his typical tight jeans. His black bracelets were still in his apartment and knowing he had the scars on his arms, I tossed him his hoodie.

"Thanks." He shot me a small smile. "So, you bringing the person here?"

"Fuck no. I don't bring people I question to the place I live."

He nodded and zipped his hoodie half way up his chest. "So, where we going?"

Shit. I had to stand my ground with him. This was how I lived my life, making the hard choices and dealing with the consequences.

"You're not coming, Quill. You're staying here."

"That right there, that thing you're doing?" He gestured with his finger, making the number eight. "Yeah, that's not a thing I'm doing with you. I'm not one of your people."

"In fact, you are. Or have you forgotten you work for me?" I narrowed my eyes and took a step toward him. "You will obey."

"Then I quit. Now, let's go." He went to leave, so I grabbed his arm, not painfully, but enough to stop him.

"No one quits working for me. I choose when the arrangement is over and you go under my rules or in a body bag." It was just the rules I had set, but they didn't apply to Quill. His face told me he saw it as a threat.

"You're crazy if you think you're going to lord your rules over me. I like to think the second your cock went into my ass, the whole 'do as I say, you're my employee' went out the window." He shook his arm free. "Or do you fuck everyone who works for you, then when they decide to try and be even a little bit equal to you, you stomp your foot on their individuality?"

I was afraid this might happen and whether Quill wanted to admit it or not, our age gap and the choices I'd had to make in my life were exactly why he and I could never be a forever thing. The thought alone sent a piercing pain straight to my heart.

"You're acting like a child, Quill. This is why we can't work." I had to stay strong, swallow down the hurt that was creeping up. "Until this is over, you're to remain here. When it ends, so do we." With no other words, or my inability to form them, I stormed out, slamming the door behind me.

"Quill doesn't leave this house," I ordered to Nathan. "Understand me?"

"Yes, sir. Your car is in the garage waiting for you."

I knew Quill was livid, likely hurt by what I said, but my life wasn't really just mine. So many people depended on me to make the hard calls. I longed for someone to bitch about my day to, to feel the tender side of a human and them to see my vulnerabilities and burdens and love me through it all. But I was mistaken to think I could ever have that or that Quill would understand.

He may never forgive me, but at least he'd be alive to hate me.

Chapter Thirty

Quill

I stood frozen for a good two minutes. Even after I heard the elevator chime indicating Black had left, I remained stock-still. It wasn't until a knock on the door that I focused.

"I'm sorry to bother you," Nathan said. "I made some coffee if you'd like any."

The pity Nathan was showing me told the tale that he not only heard Black's and my argument, but he felt bad for me. Poor Quill getting squashed again. I was an idiot to think this would work, but Black didn't give me a chance to even explain why I should go with him. Of course, I went a little insane queen on him there, so that could be why.

"Can you get a message to Black for me?" I asked Nathan as I followed him to the kitchen for that coffee.

"Sir, I really don't want to get in the middle of everything with you two. I'm his employee and that would be overstepping and… Mr. Black is quite intimidating." He pulled two mugs down and poured as he spoke.

"Aren't you like a mean assassin or something?"

He chuckled and handed me a black coffee. Naturally, he didn't know how I took it.

"No. I work in tech for Mr. Black. I help his assassins with their missions, but I've never actually shot someone or anything."

Black left me with someone who literally couldn't defend me and he thought me going with him was dangerous?

"I see." I fixed my coffee how I wanted it and sat on the stool. "Well, the message I'd like to get to him isn't personal. It's important though."

Nathan furrowed his brow, making his bottom lip jut out a little. He was a cutie, that was for sure. "Okay."

"If the man in the apartment is my brother or one of my brother's friends, he won't get anywhere with him. My going was a sure way to get him to react."

"Assuming it's your brother, and I don't believe the person I saw matched the person by the cars, Black has ways of making people talk." His knowing smile irritated me. He knew, no, he saw that dark side of Black. One he didn't want me to see.

"Is there video on Black? On any of them while they question this guy?"

Nathan shook his head. "Black doesn't leave paper trails." He slid his mug to the side, and regarded me with as serious a face as I'd seen. "You need to realize something important, Quill, um, sir."

"Quill's fine, I rather prefer it, actually."

He gave me a half smile before composing himself. "All the people who work for Black were trained by Black. All of them. Even though some came with a skill set, he cultivated it. He made it have a twist that became their signature. Anything any of them have done, he has either done it first or does it better."

In the back of my mind, I knew Black was violent, but it was like he did his time so his days of getting his hands dirty were over. I didn't look at Black and see blood on his hands. I saw a man trying to balance the world.

Nathan was just taking a sip of his coffee when his phone chimed. "Yeah," he greeted to the caller. "Hello?" He shook his head. "Is this you, Steve? Stop fucking with me."

The hairs on the back of my neck stood on end. Nathan was smiling like it was a joke, but it was hard to explain how I knew my brother was here.

"I'm hanging up. I have no time for your games."

"Nathan," It was all I got out before I heard the ding of the elevator.

"Stay here." Nathan took out his gun, one he had never fired before.

"No, Nathan, you've never used that. Stay with me. When they come in, if it's someone bad, we'll have a better chance."

He waved me off. "I've fired it, just never killed anyone. Do as I say, Quill."

I was getting really tired of people telling me what to do. I knew things. I knew my brother. He liked to play with his food before he ate it.

Nathan wasn't going to listen to me, so I had to protect myself. If I got killed, Black would murder me.

Fucking open floor plans. I only had a minute to figure out where to hide. There was a linen hamper by the pantry closet. I knew it only had a table cloth in it because I'd tossed it in there before dinner. As quickly and quietly as I could, I slipped inside, thanking everything I was small. That was a first.

I crouched down and adjusted the table cloth over myself hoping if anyone lifted the lid, they'd see the linen and assume it was just laundry.

I hadn't seen my brother in a while. Even on the video Black showed me, I saw he had bulked up more. Just what I needed… a bigger challenge.

It was way too quiet. Please, dear God, just be another of Black's men doing rounds or something.

The sound of a shot going off made me jump and I willed my body not to shake. Fuck, I hoped Nathan got him. There was no love lost between my brother and me, and I knew if he got his hands on me, I'd be screwed.

A thud, then a moan. Shit. I tried to reach my cellphone in my pocket. I didn't know if Black had his phone on him or if he'd answer it if he saw my name come across the screen, but I had to try. It rang and rang. When it went to voice mail, I whispered.

"Black, someone's here. I'm hiding in the hamper by the pantry. I heard a shot. I don't know if Nathan is alive or if I'm about to be taken. I think you're headed toward an ambush or the whole thing was a decoy to get to me here. I don't want to tell you I told you so, but I so am. If you don't find me, or even if you do, promise me to never blame yourself. I'm not Sunshine and none of this is your fault."

I hung up and took a deep breath. I listened, but it was silent. I wanted to peek out and see, but fear kept me frozen.

"Quillion Almeida!" The sound of my brother's voice cemented the fact that Nathan was dead and I was in deep shit. "I know you're here and you know I'll find you."

My body shook, the terror of Dylan getting his hands on me sent phantom pains through my body. I knew what he was capable of and I also knew he was madder than he'd ever been at me.

"I don't need or want your fucking money, Quill. I got paid to make you disappear." His laugh was laced with vengeance. "You went and pissed off the wrong people this time, little brother."

If we wondered if the Sterlings had hired him, he just confirmed it in so many words.

"I don't have all the time in the world, so why don't you make it easier on yourself by coming out now. I promise not to hurt you too badly if you just come out."

I could hear him rustling about, opening cabinets, doors, and such. His voice got softer and louder, indicating he was moving around the house.

"Where the fuck are you!" he shouted, the anger I knew all too well coming through loud and clear.

He stood right beside the hamper and the sound of the cabinet beside me slamming shut made me flinch.

"Maybe Black took him with him?" Another voice I didn't recognize said.

"Why'd he do that? He already had that shitty doppelganger hanging out at his apartment."

The unrecognizable voice spoke again. "Don't you think it's a little odd he left Quill here protected by one inept guy inside? Quill's the reason we're all doing any of this, that and the money, it just don't sit right with me."

"No one asked you," my brother said. "Black isn't as smart as he likes people to believe he is. I know my brother is here and I will fucking find him."

Chapter Thirty-One

Black

I waited in the car while Team X grabbed the guy in the apartment building. I instructed them to bring him to my car. My mind kept drifting to Quill, but I shook it off as quickly as I could and tried to focus on the task at hand.

Sometime later, there was a knock on my window and Jaclyn stood with a scrawny man in her grip. I unlocked the door and she opened it, tossed him in, and slid in beside him. Her gun pointed at him, daring him to move.

"Before you speak and start saying stupid shit, let me introduce myself to you." He narrowed his eyes but kept his mouth shut. "My name is Black. I run an assassin organization. By the looks of you, someone likely paid you a good fee to come here tonight to play decoy. Am I right?" He shook his head, his gaze shifting between me and Jaclyn's gun. "Don't pay her any mind, she won't kill you unless I order it."

The guy opened his mouth and shut it.

"What's your name?"

"Henry. I'm nineteen. I was just sleeping under a bridge, some guy asked if I'd like to make some quick cash. Said I just had to sneak in a window and walk down a hall and out a door. That's all."

He was dirty, didn't smell so nice, his hair stringy and oily. He had been on the streets a long time without a shower and by the hollowed-out cheeks, no doubt he was hungry.

"Who was the person who you spoke with under the bridge?"

My phone dinged, indicating I had a voicemail but I ignored it, waiting for Henry's answer.

"I don't know his name, wore a white hoodie, gave me fifty right there just for me to hear him out. He seemed legit about the offer and it was simple enough."

"You're an idiot," I said as I massaged my temples. "You didn't think maybe it was too simple?"

"How am I the idiot? You came here for me and you don't seem too surprised to find me." The boy had gumption, but I had no tolerance.

"I already have one moody man in my life, I don't need another." In one fluid motion, I grabbed the small knife from inside my jacket and jammed it into Henry's hand and through the upholstery.

His scream was loud in the confines of the car, like nails on a chalkboard.

"I have four knives, Henry." I raised my brows. "Now, tell me what you know. Don't bullshit me."

Henry was hysterical, screaming to take him to a hospital. I couldn't reason with him like this.

"Jaclyn, take him to the van, get him cleaned up." I spoke louder so Henry could hear me. "We can start again soon."

After he was wrangled out, I laid my head back against the seat; silence was golden indeed. Taking a moment before I went to the van, I checked my voicemail. The sound of Quill's terrified voice sent ice through my veins. Even if Nathan was shot, the others would surely handle it. Why was he hiding? How'd anyone get inside the house at all?

"Steve," I hollered as I opened the door. He stood beside the van smoking a cigarette. "You sent team Y to my home with Nathan, right?"

"Of course, why?"

"Quill called, Nathan's dead and they're in the house. Locate Team Y. Jaclyn, secure Henry. We need to get back to the house immediately."

Getting one past me wasn't a common thing. *Had Quill fucked with my concentration? What the Hell was going on?*

We were five minutes from my house when Steve called. "What do you got?"

"No answer from Team Y, Sir. Cameras outside your house only showed a car pulling up and two men exiting the vehicle. How they got in, I don't know."

Fuck, fuck, fuck. "Drive faster," I ordered, and the car zoomed up the hill toward my house.

There was no car in the driveway when we pulled up and I could only hope it was because they couldn't find Quill, gave up, and left.

"Stay in the car, sir," my driver ordered, but fuck that. I grabbed my gun from the small compartment in my car and got out. "Sir!"

"I give the orders, not you, now move."

Leaving no room for argument, five of us walked down the garage. No signs of forced entry. It was like someone had let them in, but that was impossible. Steve and Leo went up the elevator while Jaclyn, my driver, and I took the emergency stairs.

Jaclyn pushed the door open, gun at the ready. It was eerily silent. No Christmas carols playing, no aroma of chocolate, cookies, or popcorn. All things I'd grown accustomed to with having Quill here the last few days.

We rounded the corner to the living room where Nathan's body lay dead in front of the Christmas tree. Blood had flowed toward the skirt, saturating it.

I gestured two to go down the hall to the master bedroom and one to watch my back while Leo and I went into the kitchen.

Dishes laid on the floor in a million pieces, pots and pans were thrown across the room, shattering tiles in the wall. The hamper stood in place, untouched. God, please let him be in there…. Alive.

Leo pointed the gun at the hamper, just as a precaution, allowing me to slip mine in my belt and slowly lift the lid.

Linen. It was all I saw at first, then it trembled. The linen trembled.

"Quill," I whispered like I would if I were talking to a scared animal. "It's Black, baby, you're safe."

The fabric slid and his gunmetal gray hair was what I saw first, then his green, glistening eyes on the verge of tears. His lip wobbled and shakily, he lifted his arms to me. I didn't hesitate a second, grabbing him, pulling him out, and cradling him as close to me as possible.

"Shh, it's okay. I got you, you're safe." I thought he'd cry and sob, but there was nothing. Not a whimper. "Quill, baby, say something."

His grip loosened, but he stayed wrapped around me. Eyes surveyed the trashed kitchen. I knew when he froze that he saw Nathan by the tree.

"I'm so sorry, Quill. I thought Team Y was watching the house. We can't locate them. I…" He pressed a slim finger against my lips.

"You won't, they're dead. Nathan's dead. He won't stop, he can't." Quill spoke apathetically.

"How do you know?" Leo asked, lowering his gun but staying vigilant.

In the same detached tone, Quill answered, "He didn't find me. I heard him screaming. I thought for sure he'd find me, and if he had more time, I'm sure he would've. As he searched, he talked. Told me the Sterlings were quite the powerful family. Talked about how they'd dismantle the Hart family and make this city theirs. He went on about their connections and how the Sterlings' people taking out your team was easier than breathing. Even had tech people to get through your security systems."

I didn't like the vacancy in his green eyes. It was like he went into his own safe headspace to avoid feeling.

I couldn't wait for Poe to get his head out of his ass. I needed all the information on the Sterlings that I could get. I knew Teddy meditated with him, but Bill seemed to know him more. I didn't want to talk to Bill.

"Leo, get Christopher Manos on the phone. Use my cell, he won't pick up for you. He's the number that is under CM." Keeping my grip tight on Quill, I reached in my pocket and handed my phone to Leo. "Put it on speaker."

It rang three times before he answered. "I thought we were square, Black." He was brusque, a tone I'd come to associate with the mob boss.

"I wish more than you know that I never had to hear your voice again."

There was a chuckle on the other end, no doubt Christopher's husband, Snow.

"Why are you calling me at, fuck, Black, it's two in the morning. What the hell do you want... wait. Are you in jail? No way am I going near that."

He couldn't see me roll my eyes, but it was a reflex when it came to him. "No, you have a connection I can't seem to wrangle in but need desperately."

"Who?" There was rustling, likely bed sheets. It was two in the morning, I woke him up.

"Poe."

"He isn't my connection, he's Snow's friend, and while he seems to have a mysterious power about him, he's not an asshole. He clearly knows you and what you do and realizes you're a liability and wants nothing to do with you. Have you thought about..." Christopher was interrupted and the sound of muffled voices arguing sounded through the kitchen.

Quill turned, eyes on the phone like he just realized we were on a call.

"Black? Hi, it's Snow. Don't listen to my acerbic husband. I'm sure deep down past your murderous heart, you're a real prince." Christopher's chuckle came through the phone. "Now, why do you need Poe?"

I started at the beginning, told them everything. Quill didn't react much when I reiterated the things Dylan had done to him, or Ronnie. But by the time I was done, you could've heard a pin drop.

"Poe refused to help you?" Snow asked.

"Yes, but he didn't have a lot of this info. I emailed him again, explaining, but he hasn't answered me and after tonight, I can't wait for him."

Their voices were muffled again, I couldn't make it all out. But it sounded like whatever Snow wanted, he was getting.

"Black, I am calling Poe right after I hang up with you. I am telling him to get his ass over to my house immediately. I suggest you get your bundle of brave in a car and head this way too. Your place isn't safe anyway, so get hoppin'," Snow said with a snap of his fingers.

"How do you know Poe will show up at your house?" I asked as I gestured Leo and the others to get things ready for a move.

Christopher's laugh was booming. "You clearly don't know my husband. Get a move on, Black, you heard the boss."

Jaclyn found Lady Whiskers hiding in the closet in my bedroom and snagged all her belongings while Steve got Quill and my things. We were off and on our way in under fifteen minutes.

Quill telling me they had a tech guy made my next call inevitable. It rang once before he picked up.

"Lee, I need you."

Chapter Thirty-Two

Quill

It felt like I was underwater. I moved slowly, words weren't understandable. My vision was blurring. I knew the place I was inside my head, I went there often in my life. It was my safe place where the pain took longer to find me. I could smell Black, hear him, and feel him. I wanted to scream for him to pull me out, but he just held me.

I could see the lights overhead rushing past. The skylight in the car. Black's secure, warm arms cradled me, keeping my pieces from breaking apart. We were going somewhere safe, he said, but wasn't I supposed to be safe where Black was? I hoped he didn't feel guilty for things, I'd hate that.

"We are staying with you, sir." Jaclyn was speaking and the soft meows I was hearing told me Lady Whiskers was here. Oh god, how did I forget about her through all this? I was a terrible pet owner.

"We will figure everything out. We're here. Leo, take point on this. I need to stay with Quill."

Black slid out of the car. I felt every jolt, every step he took. I knew he was climbing stairs and the cold of the night turned to warmth. And Black's scent mingled with various others. *Where were we?*

"Do you need me to call the doctor?" A voice that seemed familiar asked, but I couldn't make it out.

"No, he isn't hurt. I think he's in a state. I knew someone who told me about it once. A place to keep him away from the reality of the moment. He'll come out of it on his own, I know it." Black spoke with so much certainty, I wanted to kiss his lips, thank him for being my prince if just for a moment.

"Okay, do you want to lay him down somewhere?" a woman asked softly, and I felt fingers thread through my hair.

"No, I'll keep him close."

"Come this way." That voice I knew, it was Bill. Why was Bill here? Was Mace here too?

"Really. Snow? You set me up?" I tilted my head slightly to see the room. A man with long, black hair, dark glasses, paper white skin, and dressed in a long winter coat stood in front of an elven looking man with the whitest hair and most piercing blue eyes I'd ever seen. It was like they were on fire.

"Yeah, well, Poe, you're sort of being a jerk lately. Black here asked for help, you said no, and now that is what happened." Those eyes were homed in on me. "Oh, and look, the bundle of brave is awake."

"Quill?" I lifted my chin to gaze at Black as he sat down. "You hear me?" I nodded and his worried face morphed into the sun. So bright and happy. "Oh sweet god, you had me so afraid." He pressed his lips to mine and it was like life was being pushed into me.

"I didn't come here to watch a make out session," Poe said.

"I don't remember you being an asshole. When did this happen?" Bill said as he came into view. I couldn't see Mace anywhere, so he must not be around.

"I helped you, show some gratitude." Poe pointed at Bill, it was hard to read Poe's emotions with those dark glasses.

"You also told me Mr. Hart liked balance. How is that fucking balance?" Bill gestured toward me. "Quill never hurt a soul, yet he's being tortured by a big ass family that wants to bury the Harts and you're all, 'pardon me while I have a spot of tea and a crumpet or whatever'. Get to being what you're supposed to be!"

"Okay," Poe's hands were on is hips, his lip twitched. "First,

I'm not British, so I don't even know what that was. Second, what am I supposed to be?"

"The gatekeeper or whatever. Aren't you even interested in why the Sterling family wants to destroy your boss?"

Poe's attention went right to me and Black. "Fine, you need inside which vault?"

"All of them," Black said.

"All? Are you crazy?" Poe removed his glasses, squinting at the light.

"I don't know where to start. If it's just me you're letting in there, then I will need your help. Finding everything I need to understand why Quill's charges against Ronald would garner so much violence toward him."

I was able to shift off Black's lap, but he didn't unclasp our hands.

"I will get people on it while you're looking under City Hall."

Black's nostrils flared, his gray eyes shined with contempt. "Understand one thing, Poe. I am going to end that family, and Dylan Almeida. For the sake of the Hart family's future and the future of Haven Hart, you're going to let me do it and let me get away with it. Do I make myself clear?"

I took the moment to see all the faces in the room. Bill, and Christopher Manos, which meant the white-haired man who sat on his lap had to be Snow, his husband. A few of Black and Christopher's people were scattered around. Poe stood in the center like the ringleader of this fucked up lethal circus. Everyone waited for his answer.

"You argue a tough case, Black. But if what you say about the Sterlings is true, if they are trying to wipe out the Hart family, then yes, I will help you." He waved a dismissive hand. "What you do with Dylan, I don't care. He has no value and is inconsequential to the city or the Hart family."

With a flick of Poe's wrist, he'd okayed my brother's murder and I felt relief. I wanted him gone. I needed him to go away or I'd never get to live my life without fear. I knew Black would be able to prove to Poe that the Sterlings were bad news.

"Are you going to help us?" My voice sounded rough, like I hadn't spoken in weeks. Jaclyn rushed a glass of water to me, which I guzzled and wiped my mouth with the back of my hand.

"Will who help you? I already said I would," Poe answered me, confusion in his deep, dark eyes.

"Not you." I pointed to Snow and Christopher. "You. Will you help me… us?"

Snow whispered something in Christopher's ear, which made him roll his eyes and Snow smile.

"I don't do something for nothing, Quill," Christopher said. "Someday, I will call in this favor."

I was okay with that. "I understand."

They all talked for a while and Christopher commented on how we should all get a few hours' sleep before the sun officially rose.

A woman named Maggie showed us to a room we'd be staying in for the night. It was quite lovely and even had a tiny Christmas tree in it. Everything was oak and burgundy, but I was too exhausted to notice much more than that. Steve dropped our bags in the room and told Black he and Christopher's men would be working out shifts and to call if we needed anything.

I didn't feel scared in the Manos' house, but then again, I wasn't afraid inside Black's home either… until I was.

"Will you take a shower with me?" Black asked as he stood before me. Sadness and worry warred inside my soul and my heart ached with the need to feel anything else but that. I took Black's hand and followed him to the bathroom.

We stripped in silence, every time I divested another piece of clothing, I'd chance a glance at Black and sure enough, his attention was fully on me.

When the water was warm, Black stepped in. He gave me a minute and I needed it. I had to collect myself. When Dylan was in the house and I thought any second he'd find me, I shut myself away in my safe place. It was easy to go there, but hard to step back into reality.

I opened the glass door and lust slammed into me as I took in the sight. Lean rivers of water meandered down his body, detouring to crevices, and I swore it started steaming when it glided down his cock. His normally golden and slightly silver hair was dark under the water and the weight had made it look so much longer, it reached the top of his perfect ass.

"I don't mind being gawked at by you, but I'd like to get out of here before I turn into a prune." The slight humor in his tone relaxed me, and when we locked gazes, the safety I was desperate to cling to was found.

I stepped in behind him. Without hesitation, I wrapped my arms around his stomach and rested my head against his back. I only reached the middle of it, his hair was silky and his warmth was heaven.

When his large hand covered mine against his abdomen and he just let us be like this for a moment, I was grateful. I had given up in believing in a happily ever after and Black made it really clear when this was over, we were over. But a part of me, ever so small, wouldn't extinguish the hope that he wouldn't let me go. I didn't want him to.

Black turned and his chest hair rubbed against my nose. My chin was just below his pecs, and knowing he was blocking the water from hitting my eyes, I looked up at him. His wet thumb brushed against my cheek and his gaze was flickering with so many emotions, I couldn't stay pinned on just one.

"I'm sorry, Quill," his deep voice rumbled, and I was about to interrupt him when that thumb covered my lips. "Let me finish."

He plucked the washcloth off the shower bar and began

soaping it up while he spoke. "I heard your voicemail, telling me no matter what I was walking into, not to blame myself." He shook his head, then tenderly lifted my arm and began washing me.

"You can never ask a person how to feel, Quill, and I knew before I got there, no matter what I did in fact find, I was going to blame myself."

I hated he was blaming himself at all.

"Under normal circumstances, you staying behind was the safer, smarter option. But had I listened to you, none of this would have happened. We would have talked to the guy being used as a decoy and figured it out, and might have been a step ahead of your brother and the Sterlings."

When I was all lathered, he guided me under the water, the water and suds sluiced off my body and he had me turn around.

"I've been doing this for many years and I know better. I blamed you as a distraction, and I may not be wrong there, but I am so good at my job, you should have never been an obstacle in getting this done correctly."

The timbre of his voice and the feel of his fingers as he washed my hair was sending goosebumps all over my skin. I hated hearing him being so hard on himself, but maybe he needed to vent.

"When I first had my assassin organization piggyback over my security business, I was hell-bent on finding every piece of shit in the world and destroying them. I killed hundreds of people, Quill, hundreds. I stopped counting. I took money from grieving families and ended the ones causing their suffering." He turned me to face him and pushed my head back so the water could rinse off the shampoo. Then he did the same with the conditioner, all the while telling me this story.

"I turned into a monster and then turned others into the same thing. Blackmailing them in a sense to kill for me, for my empire."

After I was completely clean, I leaned against the shower wall while Black washed himself and talked.

"I tried to only kill those deserving, but many times, I had offers to take out girls who said no on a date, or a man who gave someone's sister herpes." He rolled his eyes. "That isn't what I do and I started wondering how these things were trickling into my company. So, I stepped away from the actual killing and grabbed my business by the balls and secured it. Had the most trusted around me. I built a solid life. Sinful, yes, but righteous. That's what I told myself with every kill."

I itched to touch and soothe him, but he was stripping the last of his secrets away, allowing me to see him bare.

"When that mole infiltrated my organization, I felt I was starting to lose my edge. I mean, I should have seen it coming sooner. She should have never been able to get as deep inside as she did. It was the first time in years I killed again."

He shut the water off, opened the shower door, and grabbed the two towels hanging on the warming bar. He opened one and I snuggled into it and him.

"With what happened with you tonight, with this whole thing going left and right, up and down. It was too reminiscent of when Emma broke down my walls and tried to pry my life from me." Black took a deep breath and I felt a slight tremble in his embrace before he continued. "Then I saw the hamper and…" He swallowed loudly. "When I lifted the lid, I kept seeing Sunshine and hoped what I found wasn't a repeat."

We stood like that for a moment in silence. I let his words sink in. We broke apart slowly and after his towel was wrapped around his waist, we went back into the bedroom where we pulled the sheets back, dropped the towels, and slid naked under the silk.

"My life is full of demons I've created, Quill. If you stay, I fear they will consume you." He lifted my chin so our gazes met. "I don't get to walk away from this. It's who I am until I die. I can't ask anyone to take on my nightmares."

All the residual feelings that were weighing me down vanished. In the vulnerability of Terrance Black's eyes, I knew I held all the power for once.

"You're not asking me, Black. I'm not anywhere I don't want to be. Besides, my nightmares have been looking for dancing partners for years."

Chapter Thirty-Three

Black

It felt like Quill and I had just closed our eyes before someone, and likely a very dead someone, came barreling into the room.

"Black," Steve yelled as he turned the light on. Quill whimpered and pulled the comforter over his head.

"Why the hell are you barging in here at…?" The clock on my phone read nine. "Oh. Well, what is it?"

Steve went to the bedside table, opened the drawer, and took out the remote. "Look!"

The TV came to life, and live and in HD stood Bartholomew Sterling behind a podium. A press conference was well under way, but the caption on the screen made it feel like lava was coursing through my veins. "Bartholomew Sterling Announces His Run For Mayor of Haven Hart."

"I wanted to give the good people of Haven Hart a gift this Christmas and while I will of course do my usual charities, I wanted to get into a seat where I could begin to spread this good cheer through the government," Bartholomew said.

"Are you saying being mayor is only a stepping stone for you, Mr. Sterling?" a reporter asked.

"I'd say so, Cindy. I often am asked to please help make Haven Hart better. It's fallen into such despair, well hidden by the Hart family for sure, but while you can paint over a crappy foundation, it's still going to crumble eventually. We need more than Band-Aid solutions and I want to help make this city strong again. And who knows, maybe bring it all the way to the White House."

"Doesn't that say a lot," Quill said softly. "Charges against his son would taint his election."

"It has to be even more than that. Bartholomew would throw his son under a bus and claim he had the balls to do what was right for the city no matter the pain it's caused his bloodline," I said, gritted my teeth as I spoke.

"Has everyone seen this?" I asked Steve.

"They are all meeting in Mr. Manos' study in thirty minutes."

I dismissed Steve, and Quill and I hurried to dress and get downstairs. We weren't the last to arrive, but Christopher, Snow, and even Poe were there. I didn't know if he stayed the night or not. Seeing as we had been at Christopher's at three in the morning, I chose the former.

"Morning, Black. By the anger rippling from your presence, I take it you've seen the news?" Poe asked as he sipped what looked like tea.

"I'm surprised you're not more upset. He tore Haven Hart apart."

He shrugged. "Politicians often fabricate the truth, twist the ropes and such. Not surprising. It's been a tactic many mayors, congressmen, senators, and such have used. But while we all were sleeping, I took it upon myself to have some people dig in the vaults. I felt we were running out of time and, well, they found something."

Maggie came in with more coffee and danishes. We all settled in and listened while Poe explained what he had found.

"Bartholomew Sterling is the son of one Gregor Sterling. Gregor sadly passed away a few years ago, suspiciously so, it seems. I don't know if Gregor had inclinations his grandson was going to be a less than stellar citizen or if he knew his son went through money like water, but he made his wishes air tight." Poe handed me a file and a duplicate looking one to Christopher.

"A trust fund was set up for Ronald with a very interesting clause."

We all read in silence. Quill gasped, getting to it before me, clearly.

"That's right, Quill," Poe said. "On Ronald's thirtieth birthday, he will be able to access his trust fund. The grand number is seventy-five million dollars." He chuckled darkly. "Ronald turns thirty next year. The stipulation being Ronald isn't convicted of any, and I mean any, crimes."

Poe handed Christopher and me another piece of paper. "Just in time, too, because Bartholomew Sterling is just about bankrupt."

"Holy shit," Quill said loudly with a chuckle.

"Wait, what happens to the money if Ronald is found guilty and loses his trust fund?" Christopher asked a great question I bet I knew the answer to.

"Ahh yes, and so that circle is complete." He gestured to Gregor's will. "Read on."

We did, things about boats and such, and then there it was.

"Everything gets handed to the Hart family to disburse to families in need all over the city?" I couldn't believe it even as I said it out loud. "That's why Bartholomew wants to take down the Hart family, and Quill. Both are road blocks to him getting that money."

"Bingo!" Poe pointed at me like I guessed the winning answer.

"Do you agree that the case has been proven, Poe, that the Sterlings are hurting this city and your beloved Hart heir?" Quill asked, and a brief darkness shadowed Poe's face at the word beloved.

"I would say so, Quill."

"I no longer have need to get into your precious vaults, Poe, but Quill's hearing is fast approaching."

All eyes were on Quill.

"I can stay here if it's okay with Mr. Manos…"

"It's fine with him," Snow interrupted, earning a few laughs.

"Okay, then that's settled. You have the Christmas ball with Lana tonight. Go, maybe you'll see him there and can intimidate him with your presence."

I had forgotten about the ball, damn.

"It will be great, Black. Quill and I are gonna play with his kitty and talk. I will keep him busy. It seems to be what I do when your men get their men into trouble." Snow lifted a silvery white eyebrow.

I knew he was referring to Teddy when Riordan had done the whole fake death thing. He stayed here and Snow wasn't very keen on giving Riordan a second chance on Teddy's behalf.

When Riordan had told me he wanted to get Teddy back and his plan on embarrassing himself at Fredrick's Park in a huge pink bunny costume, I thought he was insane, but I helped him anyway. Looking over at Quill, I wondered if I would do something like that for him.

"It's settled then," Quill said, shaking me out of my daydream.

"He's got to be getting desperate," Christopher said. "If the hearing is so close, he will want Quill to drop the charges or not show up. He'd settle for either."

"Why not just drop the charges?" Jaclyn asked from her spot near the window.

"Because it's the stipulation for him not getting that money. If he dies, it goes to Bartholomew according to this will. If he's convicted, it goes to the Hart family," Poe answered her.

"Gotta say, I'm surprised dear old dad hasn't killed his son," Quill muttered.

"It would shroud his family in doubt. Bartholomew isn't a stupid man. He has a stupid son however, and while his son's murder could now conceivably earn him pity votes and secure the money, it would be too easy for him. He may be readying for a plan B." Poe sat beside Steve as he finished his tea. "Come next week, if those charges aren't dropped, we very well may find Ronald's dead body on the news."

"Who do you think hired Dylan, Bartholomew or Ronald?" Snow asked.

"The who doesn't matter, it was likely a last-ditch effort. So things are going to be dangerous for the next forty-eight hours. If Quill is staying here, keep this place on lockdown," Poe said as he turned to Christopher and Snow. "Where's Simon?"

"He and his friend CeCe are on a school trip, some nature's classroom thing. He left last night after school. He's set to return Sunday afternoon, so this needs to be done before he returns," Christopher ordered.

We all went about the day coming up with plans and plans for our plans. Christopher Manos worked a lot like I did in the fact he like alphabet plans. B, C, D, and so on.

It was five o'clock when Quill told me I had to get ready. Steve had run out to get my suit, and I dressed while Quill lay on the bed watching me.

"I'm going to be fine. Even if anyone got in here, Snow is terrifying." He chuckled, but I was having a hard time finding it humorous.

"When this is all over, I'm teaching you self-defense. I see you as a survivor, not a victim, believe that, but you need to know how to defend yourself."

Quill sat up, feet tucked under his butt, hands on either side of his legs. With his head cocked to the right, he looked so young, but there was a determination in his gaze that made my dick come alive.

"Thought you said when this was over, we were over?"

Ahh... "I don't know I have a choice in the matter anymore,

Quill." I slipped my jacket on and walked toward the bed. As soon as I was close enough, Quill lifted, wrapping his arms around my neck.

"How's that?"

"My head and my heart are joining forces. They're unstoppable beasts."

He chuckled into my kiss and took it so slow. I hated leaving him tonight to deal with this ball, but understood the need to be seen. To show Bartholomew I was unaffected by his stupid attempts. Not to mention, Lana would be so sad to miss it.

It was going to be a long night. But if it went the way I hoped, it would be the beginning of the end for the Sterling family.

Chapter Thirty-Four

Quill

The first two hours after Black left, Snow seemed to think he had to give me a grand tour, play two board games, and excitedly tell me that the Hallmark Channel was showing marathon Christmas movies and that was what we were going to be doing all night. I didn't mind, really. It did make me miss Mel though. She was my best friend and we often vegged on the couch while I played video games or we watched cheesy romance movies.

I was able to text her, letting her know I was okay, and she told me she missed me and was eager to have this over with. Ronnie hadn't come back into Quirks and Perks and she hadn't bumped into Dylan anywhere. I was happy about that.

"I don't know, that guy's arrogance is kind of sexy. I mean, the farm boy is totally hot, but I'm having issues with her choices," Snow said as he chomped on popcorn. We were on movie two and I was half watching it.

"Maybe she's tired of rich assholes?" I asked, garnering a shrug from him.

"Sometimes those assholes are worth it." He nudged my arm and there was no question he was talking about his husband. My own mind went to Black. He was nothing like I thought he'd be.

Sure, Black was an asshole. He had confidence, but he was also vulnerable in a lot of ways. That night he told me about Sunshine and sobbed without shame told me more about the man than years with him could. Christopher Manos, to an outsider, seemed sturdy, rich, unstoppable, and unaffected. But I was sure Snow saw a side of him nobody else was privy to. I wanted that with someone. And in that moment, while watching silly Christmas romances, I vowed to make Black mine. I wouldn't let him push me away when this was over. I knew he was wishy-washy over it all, but I'd show him I was his person.

"Not buying it, Susan," Snow shouted at the TV, making me laugh.

With Lady Whiskers curled in my lap, I spent the rest of my evening with Snow, who did an amazing job of keeping my mind occupied. I could see it in his eyes, he knew I wasn't all here, but he never forced me to talk about it and for that, I was grateful.

Christopher came in and talked with us for a while until Snow shushed him and told him to go away so he could hear the cheesy dialog.

At eleven, my eyes were starting to droop. I couldn't watch anymore and I took Lady Whiskers upstairs to the bedroom. I must have crashed, because the next thing I knew, the sun was streaming through the windows. I reached over for Black only to hit cold emptiness. I didn't know if he was up or what was going on. When I opened the door, the cat ran out, likely looking for her food. Lisa, one of Christopher's staff, adored Lady and probably had her food waiting for her.

I quickly washed, dressed, and went downstairs. I gravitated toward the voices coming from the kitchen. Inside, Snow, Christopher, Maggie, and a few others were sitting down, eating.

"Morning," I mumbled as I took the hot mug offered to me. "Thank you, Maggie."

"Have a seat, I made a breakfast casserole. I'll plate you some."

At the table, no one looked bothered with the fact that Black wasn't here.

"Has anyone seen or heard from Black?" I asked.

That was when I noticed none of Black's people were here

and the room was thick with suspicious behavior. The silence was very telling.

"What?" I searched their faces, but no one was talking. Not even Snow. "Fine, then I'll just be heading back to my place. Clearly, all is well with the world and I can return home?"

Christopher let out a long, frustrated breath. "No, you can't leave. Black didn't return last night, but he contacted me. He's dealing with this situation, you need to let him. He said when it was all over, he'd come get you and you'd be free to do or go wherever you want."

"He went to take care of everything?" Christopher nodded and went back to reading his paper. *Who reads the newspaper anymore?* "What happened at the ball? I thought there was a plan in place?"

"There was and it's being executed." Christopher shrugged like he didn't have a care in the world.

"You promised to help us!" I slammed my hands on the table, Christopher's dark eyes snapped to mine and the glare sent a scary shiver through my body. It wasn't like when Black looked at me. I knew Black would never harm me, but Christopher had zero attachment to me.

"Sit," he snapped. "I am helping, just because in this exact moment I'm eating breakfast doesn't mean I'm not, or have not, been keeping up with my promise."

"Why am I not in the know?" I sat down as asked and everyone in the kitchen seemed to relax.

"Maybe because you were sleeping and just got in here exactly two minutes ago?" Christopher said as he folded the paper. "What do you want to know?"

"Everything."

After breakfast, all of Christopher's people, Snow, and myself went into his study. I wasn't nervous exactly, but I was curious as to why, after Black said he wanted me in the know, I did not understand what was going on. If Black was in danger, I was sure someone would have awakened me and let me know.

"Black called me at around midnight. I had been in contact with him periodically, but things were very uneventful. Bartholomew Sterling did, in fact, show up, but was a beacon for people and therefore, getting to him proved to be difficult." Christopher held up his pointer. "But not impossible."

Christopher sat at his desk while Snow sat in a wingback chair beside it, engrossed in listening to his husband, and I wondered if he was hearing it for the first time.

"There were over five hundred people at the ball and..."

"Five hundred and twenty-two," Snow interrupted.

"Okay, five hundred and twenty-two," Christopher said, amusement in his tone. "But when Bartholomew saw Black, it seemed to be all the man could see. And when Black went into the bathroom, Bartholomew followed."

"Is this going to get pervy?" Snow asked, but Christopher waved him off.

"This was where Bartholomew made his first mistake. It was part of Black's plan the entire time. The bathrooms were near the back exits of the facility the ball was being held at, so when Bartholomew entered, so did Black's men. Lee was able to force a brownout of sorts and, when that happened, Black's men took Bartholomew out the back after sedating him."

"Wait, Lee's back?" I didn't know this, but was glad. Lee was wicked smart and with the Sterlings having so much help in the technology department, we needed him.

"He is. Then Black went back out and enjoyed the rest of the ball. Black said there was some buzz about his disappearing from the ball, but his wife seemed to get a little too drunk and wasn't worried about it much."

"So, Black is with Bartholomew right now?"

Christopher nodded. "Yes."

All of that made sense. I was glad Black had his men with him and he was safe.

"Black is going to end this, Quill. Be sure the man that comes through those doors when it's over is a man you're going to be able to accept." Christopher's gaze was intense.

"I'm sure," I answered without any hesitation.

Chapter Thirty-Five

Black

With my bow tie long gone, the first three buttons of my white dress shirt unbuttoned, and exhaustion settling in my bones, I sat across the table from Bartholomew Sterling. His eyes were piercing me with hatred and I didn't give one shit about it.

"You'll never be mayor, Bart. Quill will not drop the charges, your son will be convicted, and you'll never get your fucking hands on your son's money, then your entire family will cease to be an issue for Quill or the Hart family." I liked reminding him of all these things throughout the night. Each time, the anger ignited something and he fought the bindings.

"I'm called in when nothing else has worked. This time, however, I'm doing this because you fucked with my world."

I was sure if he wasn't gagged, he'd have a few choice words for me. But he'd said all I wanted to hear right now. He saw Henry, the homeless kid he had hired to pretend to be Dylan, tied beside him and spit right in his face, calling him worthless. Jaclyn made sure to separate them, and I didn't think I'd have any use for the kid right now... But people like him needed a new direction, so I had Jaclyn keep an eye on him. When this was over, I'd deal with Henry.

"I kept warning you to accept the way things were, but you kept thinking you were unstoppable." I punched the table, smiling when Bartholomew jumped. "I am the unstoppable force. I am the immovable object. You are just another person thinking they can alter how things are done here in Haven Hart. But you got cocky, Bart, and made too many mistakes and pissed off too many superpowers here. That's why you're here and why I'm the last person you'll ever get to see." I placed my 9mm on the table, followed by the silencer. Bartholomew eyed them nervously.

"You've told me all I needed to know, which wasn't a lot." I twisted the silencer onto the gun. "See, there was a time you could've made this right and lived. But now," I aimed the gun at Bartholomew's head, "that moment has passed."

Bartholomew got out a screech before I gently squeezed the trigger and a perfectly placed shot went through his forehead. Blood and brain splattered against the kitchen counter of the vacant house I owned. Bartholomew's head snapped back and then forward. Crimson flowed over the table, and I stood before it reached me.

"Clean that up," I said to Leo, who got straight to work.

Bartholomew admitted to allowing his son to contact Dylan Almeida and asking him to take care of the Quill problem. Ronnie was having a hard time letting Quill go, but when threatened with having no money, the choice was easy.

Now it was time to pay Ronnie a visit. I was saving Dylan for last.

Ginger tracked down Ronnie and I changed from my tux into black pants and a black, long-sleeved shirt. Poe informed me that Bartholomew's wife filed a missing person report, but that he'd handle it. I had to trust him. Christopher messaged me that Quill had been informed and was taking all this news well. Everything was falling into place. Sure, the Sterlings had gotten the jump on me, but that only happened once. They were in my game now, playing by my rules, and I won every time.

By the time Bartholomew's body was moved and cleaned up, I got word they were approaching with Ronnie. Lee set up the TV with the video ready to go. So I made myself comfortable on the couch and enjoyed my coffee.

Ronnie struggled, of course, not enjoying being manhandled. He was a man who lived to be the alpha, but not this time.

"Welcome, Ronnie, you're just in time for the show," I said loudly to be heard over his cursing and shouts. "Take a seat." Steve pushed him down on the chair while Leo and Jaclyn tied him to it... tightly.

"What the fuck do you think you're doing? I know you know who I am, so I guess you're stupid because..." Nope. I wasn't listening to this. With a simple wave of my hand, a gag was securely placed in his mouth. Of course, he tried to talk through it, so it was time to shut him up. I clicked play on the television. When Bartholomew appeared on the screen, Ronnie shut up immediately.

He watched his father and I watched him as I sipped my coffee. The entire confession, how he admitted he'd kill his own son for that money. Ronnie watched as his father admitted to handing it all over to Ronnie to deal with Quill and how he thought his son was a huge liability. I rolled my eyes when he cried, realizing he was no more than a cash cow for his father.

The video ended when I shot Bartholomew, killing him. And it was in that second, Ronnie realized his fate.

"You had a piece of shit father. You and probably sixty percent of the population. It's the facts of life, Ronnie." I pointed to the TV. Bartholomew's face frozen and lifeless was on the screen. "He got off easy because he never laid a finger on Quill. You however did, repeatedly. So allow me to show you what it feels like to be on the other end of those fists of yours."

I went at him for hours. By the time I was done, my knuckles ached. They were split open and bleeding. He still breathed, but barely.

"Finish him," I said as I kicked the chair over.

Steve and Leo dragged him out and Jaclyn came over with a first aid kit.

"One more left," she said as she cleaned me up.

"Best for last, I guess."

She smiled softly. "You must really love him to see this through personally, sir."

Love him? Did I? I knew I felt for Quill more than I did any other person alive... or dead.

"Sorry, I didn't mean to overstep," she said as she wrapped my knuckles.

"Did we locate Dylan?" I opted to ignore her and stay in the headspace of the job.

"Not yet, sir. But Lee is going through Ronnie's phone now. He was able to vocally manipulate his voice to sound like Ronnie. He's giving Dylan this location as a safe house for where Quill is. Dylan won't be able to resist."

She was right, he couldn't resist at all. With all but the bedroom light out, we heard Dylan arrive. Lee told Dylan I was off with a lead on where Ronnie's men were hiding and that Quill was at the safe house fast asleep. Dylan couldn't resist.

I rested on the bed, sitting up against the headboard, gun pointed at the door. Any second, the monster that chased Quill for years was about to come face to face with his fate. His end. Me.

"Oh Quillion!" Dylan's voice echoed through the house. Taunting, vicious. Like Quill was a play thing. It made me sick and angry. "Did you miss me?"

Oh, I wasn't going to miss.

When he opened the door, he was alone, the smile of thinking he had won vanished the second one of my bullets shattered his kneecap.

"Mother fucker!" Dylan shouted. He reached for his own gun, but I shot again, this time through his hand.

"I'll take you a piece at a time if I have to."

I rose from the bed and walked over. He sat in a pool of blood. Eyes that looked nothing like Quill's stared murderously at me.

"Many people have given me that look, Dylan. But I never wanted to end anyone quite as much as I want to end you."

I crouched down, then grabbed his gun and tossed it on the bed.

"You're Black," he said as he gasped for air. There was a lot of blood. No doubt, he was feeling it.

"I am. And you're Dylan, his piece of shit brother."

He screamed as I applied pressure to his wounded knee. "Did Ronnie tell you who I am? Did he tell you who Quill was to me?"

"Fuck, man, stop." He tried to push away, but my grip was fierce.

"I run the most successful assassin organization in the world. Quill is the only person that matters to me. You've spent years making his life a living hell. So now, I'm going to take you there, in pieces."

By the time I was done with Dylan, he was exactly how I'd promised. He felt every shot, every stab, and every slice. He didn't go quietly, and he didn't go peacefully. He knew why he got what he deserved. And his last words were to please just kill him. It was his dying wish and I happily granted it.

My entire body vibrated as the adrenaline left me. I needed to see Quill at the same time I was afraid to look him in his color-of-the-day eyes and tell him what I'd done.

I waited until the sun rose two days later to face him. As I drove to Christopher's mansion, I hoped it wasn't to say goodbye. I knew my life was blood and violence, but Quill made the loud chaos an easy hum. For the first time ever, I needed someone. I needed him.

Chapter Thirty-Six

Quill

Christopher informed me that Black was returning. I had spent days worrying about him. I knew everyone who ever hurt me or threatened to hurt me was dead. I thought I'd feel sad knowing my brother was gone, but I didn't. I was relieved. The only person in this whole world who had the power to cause me pain ever again was Black. If he told me to go, I'd die inside.

"He's here," Christopher said as he rose from the couch and walked to the front door. I followed, stopping a few feet behind him. When he opened the door, Black stood there. His gaze met Christopher's briefly before landing on me.

I was frozen in place for just a moment, but the thaw was fast, and as soon as Christopher moved out of the way, I raced over to Black and leapt into his arms, breathing for the first time when he tightened his embrace. I could feel the air crackle, it was the feeling right before a thunderstorm. When his breath coasted over my neck, it was like I was plugged into life.

"Black," I whispered before kissing him breathless.

It was like I was in an impenetrable cocoon and it was just him and me. Every inch of me melted, feeling him love me through unspoken words and possessive touches. I didn't need the words. I felt them and they were everything I'd ever dreamed of.

"It's over," he said against my lips.

"Are we over?" I asked, knowing we weren't but still needing to hear it.

He was shaking his head before I was finished asking my question. "No, I don't want us to be."

I couldn't believe it. I had wished my whole life for a fairytale ending. For my prince to come save me from my life, and I got so much more than a prince or a knight, I got the king.

As much as I wanted to fall to the floor and make love to my king, I knew we couldn't. I needed to make sure everything that happened wouldn't come back to bite Black in the ass, ever.

Poe arrived an hour later and Black had a chance to change and get comfortable before the inquisition.

"Mrs. Sterling will be given the seventy-five million dollars to tell the press a very believable story about her husband stealing their son's trust fund and fleeing with his mistress. When Ronnie doesn't show up for his hearing, things will get sticky. And let's just say when he can't take it anymore and he's found in a seedy area beaten to death in an alley, well, you get it. After a few months, the shame will be too much for Mrs. Sterling and she will disappear, seventy-five million dollars richer," Poe explained.

"And you're sure she's not going to be an issue?" Christopher asked.

"Don't you worry about the matriarch, she'll be watched."

Poe didn't stay long. He thanked Black for protecting Mr. Hart and bid us all a farewell. Snow followed him out and after all the last of the details were finalized, the hour showed it was past midnight. While Black's people were running last minute sweeps over his apartment in the city, we took up Snow on his invitation to stay one last night. The gorgeous house I had made into a Christmas wonderland would need serious cleaning and I really just wanted to be in Black's arms, I didn't care where. Black and I returned to the bedroom hand in hand and lazily got ready for bed.

"Christmas is in five days," Black said as we slipped under the covers.

"Yup."

"I have this ridiculously huge apartment in the city that's devoid of any holiday cheer."

I laughed against his chest. "Is that so, Mr. Blackrose?"

"It is indeed. Happen to know of any quirky, gorgeous men who love to decorate that could come and jingle it up?"

"Hmm." My finger danced around his nipple. "I may know a guy."

"Think he can join me tomorrow…" He hesitated for a minute, and I waited patiently. "And maybe stay?"

"Stay?" I lifted my head, his silver eyes glittering. "How long?"

"I was thinking forever." It was like he was holding his breath, nervous. I couldn't believe it either, and the tickle in the pit of my stomach was pure excitement.

"I'm thinking I could be persuaded."

"I'll persuade you for as long as you need," he mumbled against my lips as he laid me on my back and spent the entire night loving every inch of my skin until I quivered. The air smelled like Black, and there wasn't any part of my body he didn't touch.

If this was my life now, then I was so glad to be wrong. It seemed I was, in fact, destined for a happily ever after.

Epilogue

ONE YEAR AND FIVE DAYS LATER
Black

"Don't you feel the difference in the embrace as the arms and the legs tangle and protect you?" Teddy was laying on our floor by the tree, trying to convince Quill that being a professional cuddler was perfect for him.

"Yeah, um, Teddy? This isn't going to be a thing for me." I watched, amused as he tried to wriggle free.

"Just breathe," Teddy said, and I turned to Riordan, who was watching the shenanigans with the same joy.

For the past year, Quill, with a lot of encouragement, had been going to therapy. The abuse he went through for so many years was festering beneath the surface. The piercings, bracelets, change of hair and eye color constantly, wasn't a quirk that was helping him find himself, it was hiding who he was. Quill Almeida was an amazing man.

He'd since kept his hair black and only wore colored contacts on Halloween when he played a very sexy devil. Quill didn't suffer from touch aversion like the therapist thought, but he wasn't a huge fan of strangers, or Teddy, wrapping themselves around him.

"I can't breathe, Teddy!"

"Let him go, babe," Riordan chuckled as he sipped his egg nog.

"Fine. I know someone who would love to cuddle with me." Teddy got up and Riordan put his egg nog down and opened his arms, only to be rebuffed as Teddy leaned into the basinet and lifted his baby girl.

"My beautiful Rosie loves her dada, don't you, my precious. Yes, you do. You let me cuddle you whenever I want, isn't that right?" He spoke to the one month old with so much enthusiasm, there wasn't a frown in the room.

"I love your cuddles too," Riordan said, feigning a pout.

"Aww, of course you do, papa." Teddy took a seat on Riordan's lap, and the three of them were a sight.

Had someone asked me if I saw Riordan being a father five years ago, I would have laughed in their face. Now, I was shocked I never saw it to begin with.

"You want that?" Quill asked as he climbed onto my lap. The fire crackled, the Christmas lights twinkled, and the speaker played Bing Crosby softly.

"Honestly?" Quill nodded, no inclination what he wanted me to say. I chose honesty. "No."

"So you won't be upset if I tell you I don't either?"

I cupped his precious face in my hands, caught breathless with the power of love I felt for this outstanding man before me.

"Not wanting children doesn't make you or me a bad person. I have you, which is more than I ever thought I'd get in this lifetime. I'm happy with you."

He pressed his candy cane flavored lips to mine and hummed.

"I'm happy with you and our dysfunctional life too."

"Okay, I'm not promising perfection. I never made egg nog cheesecake before, so good luck." Xander placed the cake on the coffee table, cut each of us pieces, then sat down and waited.

"Oh wow, this is delicious," Teddy said with the baby in his arms being fed by Riordan.

"I agree," Riordan said.

"How about you guys?" Quill took a bite, and then offered me one. The flavor exploded in my mouth. Classic eggnog and the texture was smooth.

"You nailed it, dude," Quill said as he devoured the rest of the piece.

Christmas was a time I normally spent alone. Lana had usually joined me, but this year, she was spending it with her new boyfriend. And Mel, Quill's best friend, flew to the Bahamas with her brother. Quill wanted to start a tradition of a small group of people. He and Xander hit it off last year, and they both began meditating with Teddy, Snow, and on occasion, Poe. Snow, Christopher, and Simon had their own traditions, and Poe declined. Riordan's family all flew to Ireland this year and with the new baby, neither wanted to chance such a long flight, so I invited them here.

It was uneventful, and I was loving the holiday for the first time since I had been a teenager and both my parents were alive.

"Can you come with me for a minute?" Quill asked while Riordan, Teddy, and Xander were engaged in a conversation.

"Sure."

I followed him down the hallway. Quill had liked my apartment well enough, but he said it just didn't feel like it belonged to him. So, a month later, we were moving into a house in the suburbs, where I said I'd never live.

It sat on ten acres of land with enough security to keep us safe. It had two floors, five bedrooms, three baths, a pool, and most importantly, it had Quill.

He refused to quit working at Quirks and Perks because he genuinely loved working there and he got to do it with Mel. But Joker's Sin was done and he no longer worked for me. Now he was working *with* me.

When we entered our bedroom, he shut the door.

"Everything okay?" He nodded and began unbuttoning his shirt. "Babe, believe me when I say, I want nothing more than to fuck the hell out of you, but our company… Let me go tell them to leave." I went to do just that, but he stopped me.

"No, this won't take long. Sit on the bed."

For the last week, Quill had been rebuffing me anytime I tried to have sex with him, telling me I'd understand soon.

As I sat on the bed, I watched with aching need as he slowly unbuttoned his shirt. At first, I didn't see anything. Then the shirt slid from his arms, revealing identical wings to the ones on my chest.

"Oh, Quill…"

"Wait, there's more." He turned, his back facing me. In stunning calligraphy across the top of his back, it read: From These Ashes Our Story Was Born. And it was two phoenixes rising from swirling ashes.

"Holy shit." I couldn't sit on the bed so far away from him. I spun him around until his emerald eyes were on me. "That's the most amazing gift anyone's ever given me."

"And your heart is the most amazing gift anyone's ever given to me."

As we stood there kissing each other, I felt truly alive, powerfully loved, and incredibly horny.

"Nope. I'm kicking them all out. Get your sexy ass on that bed. I'll be right back to jingle your balls."

The sound of his laughter as I speed walked down the hallway to empty the house was my most favorite music in the world.

THE END

Author's Note

Thank you for reading From These Ashes. I hope you loved it. Please feel free to leave a review on Amazon and/or Goodreads about your thoughts. I have an open door policy so feel free to email me anytime davidsonkingauthor@yahoo.com

Acknowledgements

This is the part where I tell you how this book wouldn't have been made possible without some amazing people. It's so beyond true. Let's get right to it.

To my BETA's Luna David, Annabella Michaels, and Stephanie Carrano. The fixed all the thing reader's will never know about and made it pretty.

To my editor Heidi who has endless patients with me and always pushes me that extra mile.

My proofreaders Melissa Womochil and JM Dabney for making sure all the gremlins were caught. You're awesome.

To Michelle Powell who won the character contest and brought Xander Vayne to all of you. Thank her for that one.

Also, thank you Morningstar Ashley for always knocking it out of the park with my covers, teasers, and banners. You are amazing.

There are so many to thank and so little time. My family always gets my love because they endure my freak outs as the deadline creeps up. I love your faces!

About the Author

Davidson King, always had a hope that someday her daydreams would become real-life stories. As a child, you would often find her in her own world, thinking up the most insane situations. It may have taken her awhile, but she made her dream come true with her first published work, Snow Falling.

When she's not writing you can find her blogging away on Diverse Reader, her review and promotional site. She managed to wrangle herself a husband who matched her crazy and they hatched three wonderful children.

If you were to ask her what gave her the courage to finally publish, she'd tell you it was her amazing family and friends. Support is vital in all things and when you're afraid of your dreams, it will be your cheering section that will lift you up.

Facebook Group, Author Page, Personal Page, Instagram, Amazon, Goodreads, Twitter

Printed in Great Britain
by Amazon